Praise for Deas

"The old crafters of myths and fairy tales were master psychologists. Their stories have helped countless generations to learn about power and courage, fear and loss, devotion and commitment, and above all how to be true to oneself. With *Deas and Other Imaginings*, Valerie Tarico is making a sublime and important new contribution to this ancient genre. What a gift to today's children!"

> ~**Chris Mercogliano**, Former Director of the Albany Free School in New York; author of *In Defense of Childhood: Protecting Kids' Inner Wildness, How to Grow a School, Teaching the Restless: One School's Remarkable No-Ritalin Approach to Helping Children Learn and Succeed*; and co-author of *The Love: Of the Fifth Spiritual Paradigm*.

"How captivating and inspiring are these stories and their accompanying artwork! As a child, a great deal of my moral and ethical formation evolved from immersion in fairytales, fables and myths. Indeed, my own sense of spirituality has its roots in the world of latent power made manifest through innate longing, courage, inquisitiveness, and receptivity. Through *Deas*, Dr. Tarico suspends reality, yet takes us to a place more authentic than our everyday world. It is a world where the divine child lives and where all good things are possible. This world is for adults as well as children, and it is one we can gratefully enter when reading *Deas*."

> ~**Reverend Donna Johnson**, Senior Minister at Unity Church of Fairfax, Virginia; Board Chair for Unity Worldwide Ministries; coordinator of "A Bed for Every Child" missionary work in Honduras, Costa Rica, and Peru; contributing journalist for *Contact* magazine; B.S. in Psychology and Secondary Education; and Advisor to Pinnacle Academy of Virginia, an award-winning elementary school specializing in math and technology for the future.

"You will want to read this lyrical book of parables to your child while sitting in the grass under your favorite shade tree or curled up before a roaring fire. And you will need to read it when life is hard and you begin to lose your way. *Deas* is a gift of the heart that speaks to the soul."

> ~**Bobbi Carducci**, Executive Director of Young Voices Foundation, a nationally recognized educational nonprofit established to mentor young writers; President of Community Voices Media, LLC; author of award-winning short stories; and creator of the *Story Writer* children's book series.

"Children develop a unique empathy and appreciation for ethical principles by identifying with characters in favorite stories. With luminous visual imagery and ingenious narrative dexterity, Tarico gives us stories about the development of universal wisdom. Her captivating characters – who are often children coming of age – discover essential life truths from their myriad experiences. They wrestle with extreme hardship, greed, hubris, narrow-mindedness, and vanity. Assisted by compassionate elders and their own evolving moral compasses, they learn to care for the vulnerable, face adversity with courage, and value humanitarianism in their communities."

~**Laura Kastner, Ph.D.**, Associate Professor of Psychiatry and Behavioral Sciences at the University of Washington; and co-author of *Getting to Calm: Cool-Headed Strategies for Parenting Tweens and Teens, The Launching Years: Strategies for Parenting from Senior Year to College Life,* and *The Seven Year Stretch: How Families Work Together to Grow Through Adolescence*

"*Deas* is a vibrantly illustrated book and one you don't want to miss! Not only is the prose lovely, but the artwork created by Tony Troy is entrancing and will engage children of every age. Also, the illustrations are wonderfully varied: some are dreamlike, some are intricate, and some evoke elusive yet innate archetypal urgings that are certain to inspire the young reader and capture his and her imagination."

~**Linda Trusilo, M.S.Ed.**, Master Art Teacher and Master Mentor for Montgomery County Public School System, Montgomery County, Maryland; and Adjunct Professor of Arts Integration at Towson University.

"In these wonderfully lyrical and evocative stories, Tarico takes us to unexpected conclusions about our own nature and what true wisdom and compassion really mean. Through carefully threaded, yet beautiful and poetic tales, we learn much about the nature of our own humanity, how to deal with hardship, and how to find our ethical compass. These stories will resonate with children and adults of all ages via their transcendent, universal messages."

~**Anil Singh-Molares**, Board Chair for the Compassionate Action Network, Interspiritual Chair Person for Seeds of Compassion; Co-founder of the Preeclampsia Foundation; and Recipient of a Woodrow Wilson National Fellowship Award.

Deas...
and Other Imaginings:
Ten Spiritual Folktales for Children

Written by Valerie Tarico, Ph.D.

Illustrated by Tony Troy

Published by The Oracle Institute Press, LLC
A Division of The Oracle Institute, a 501(c)(3) educational charity
1990 Battlefield Drive
Independence, Virginia 24348
www.TheOracleInstitute.org

Publisher's Cataloging-in-Publication Data

Tarico, Valerie.
   Deas-- and other imaginings : ten spiritual folktales for children / written by Valerie Tarico ; illustrated by Tony Troy.
   p. cm.
   SUMMARY: Collection of ten magical and morally challenging wisdom tales for children. The stories promote universal spiritual values, such as self-responsibility, perseverance, empathy and love.
   Audience: Ages 5-15.
   LCCN 2010929503
   ISBN-13: 9780977392940
   ISBN-10: 0977392945

   1. Tales. 2. Conduct of life--Juvenile fiction. 3. Spiritual life--Juvenile fiction. [1. Folklore. 2. Conduct of life--Fiction. 3. Spiritual life--Fiction.]   I. Troy, Tony, ill. II. Title.

PZ7.T16565Dea 2011   [Fic]
       QBI11-600188

Book design by Wordsprint
www.Wordsprint.com

Printed and bound in the U.S.

Author's Note

We often underestimate the ability of children to enjoy and absorb stories or concepts that lie at the edge of their grasp. Indeed, learning to wrestle with ideas we understand dimly – and to delight in the wrestling – is the heart of growth.

Consequently, credit for this book should go to my daughters Brynn and Marley, who taught me not to dumb things down for them. They weren't adults, to be sure, but they were almost always ready to stretch themselves. Today Brynn and Marley are relentless readers, but back then they simply had a boundless fascination with big words, magical ideas, and the mystery of faraway places. *Such muses!*

I also wish to thank my husband Brian, who believed that the tales I penciled were worth compiling into a book and sharing with others. Over the years, he and I have re-read these stories aloud to our girls, and with each reading they hear more of the underlying values – selfless love, simple delights, and quiet courage – that create a life well lived.

Traditional folktales and oral wisdom teachings have a lyrical, almost seductive pace that allows deeper insights to flow beneath the surface. These qualities create a timeless and universal appeal that often is missing in action-packed, mass-produced entertainment.

The stories collected in *Deas* aspire to this kind of ageless relevance.

Contents

The Flame

In a gray cobbled square, surrounded by gray stone buildings, under a sky of low-hanging gray clouds, a boy knelt in the sheltering corner of an old monument and built a fire. He used a bundle of sticks that he had been carrying all day, calling through the streets for a buyer, for that was his work.

The boy was thin, small for his age, with a peaked face peering out of an oversized hat made of sheepskin. The hat belonged to his older brother, who had gone south for the winter to work in the mines. "Keep this for me," he had said, both of them knowing it was a prized possession. "I'll see you after the thaw." Then he had left, with his collar turned up against the blustery autumn wind.

The boy tugged the hat down, as if he could somehow stretch it to his shoulders. He held out his hands over the little blaze, and rubbed them together. Other children his age were snug in their homes, for the winter night comes quickly, and the weather was turning. But he dared not go. "Don't bother coming home with empty pockets," his aunt had said. "Your brother's never coming back to this wretched place. I'll not feed you for nothing."

Now the boy hunched closer to the flame, wondering where he could spend the night. He thought about his small cousins, chirping for dinner like hungry birds, and his aunt bent over the stew pot. He thought of his uncle stomping in the doorway to shake off the mud and a dusting of the snow that had begun to fall, grim and bent with fatigue from driving the sheep to shelter. No, he dared not go. He held his stomach and shivered.

From among the shadowy figures that hurried through the square in the dimming light, a man appeared beside him, unfamiliar. He was a tall man, strong featured, with dark eyes and the grizzled stubble of a beard. A traveler, by the look of his long coat and his staff. "May I share your fire?" he asked. The boy hesitated. It was so small and would soon be gone. He hated to make space for anyone else, but the man must be cold too. He nodded. The man lowered a bulky pack to the ground, and the boy moved over.

For a time, the two sat in silence, watching the flame and the scattered flakes that settled on the sticks and the cobbles and their clothing. The last of the villagers had passed now, and the stillness was broken only by the boy reaching every so often for another stick from his dwindling bundle. Though he was farther from the fire than when he had it all to himself, the boy began to feel warmer sitting beside the man. *I wonder if I am dying*, he thought. He had heard that when you are dying from the cold you feel, in the end, drowsy and warm. Yet he felt alert and clear headed. He looked up at his companion.

"Are you hungry?" asked the man. He reached into his pocket and gave the boy a small loaf of bread, dark and heavy. The boy broke off a piece, and tried to give back the rest, but the man shook his head. "Eat," he said. "You will need it for your journey." *What journey?*, the boy wondered. But he didn't ask.

Time passed. The boy put the last stick on the fire. When it was almost gone, the man opened a wooden box, lined with metal. He handed it to the boy. "Put the last of the fire in here," he said. The boy looked confused, knowing that a fire can't be kept in a box. "Go ahead," said the man. "A flame may last longer and travel farther than you think." The boy did as he suggested, then closed the box and held it, peering down at the curious carvings that covered its lid. To his surprise, the box became deliciously warm. It eased the cold in his hands as the open fire had not.

The boy looked up at the man. "You are a mage," he whispered. The man's eyes creased slightly at the corners.

"I am looking for an apprentice," he said.

Hope flooded through the boy. "Are you asking me?" he said, still whispering.

"Yes," said the man.

The boy sat frozen in wonder. Then he slumped. He remembered his brother taking hold of his chin, and lifting up his wet face and making a promise: *I will come with money, and we will leave here and make a home together. We will buy some lambs and a goat …* He had clung to that promise for five long months, holding out hope when others jeered. He would hold on to it now, though it closed the only door open to him. "I cannot leave here," he said. "My brother is coming for me when the snow melts." Tears stung his eyes, and he put a hand over his face to hide them.

"Your brother will know where to find you," said the man quietly. "It is his love for you that sent me here. I met him on the Southern Road. He too shared the last of his fire. I asked him to join me. But he could not be deterred from his path to the mines, for he was determined to buy your independence along with his own. I make you this promise: I will leave a mark at your door, and though he knows not that it exists, yet he will read it and find you."

Slowly the boy lowered his hand and looked up. He looked into the eyes of the man, and believed him. "I must tell my aunt and uncle that I am going," he said. The man gathered up his pack, and the boy tucked the box inside his thin woolen jacket, pressing the warmth against him to convince himself the conversation had not been a dream. The wind was picking up, and the snow blew against their backs as they made their way through the streets.

They came finally to a wooden house on the edge of town. It stood alone, a faint light gleaming through cracks in the single shuttered window and the heavy plank door. When the man knocked, the uncle answered, opening the door slightly so that his body filled the gap, blocking the cold air and snow. "What is it?" he asked gruffly.

"I would like to take your nephew as my apprentice," the mage answered. The uncle stared at him for a moment, noticing for the first time the small figure in his shadow. He glanced down at the boy, who nodded his agreement, and then beckoned the mage into the room. The boy followed, standing behind the mage and wrapping his arms around himself, suddenly fearful. The small cousins stared up from the table, and the aunt stepped up to join the conversation, looking questioningly at her husband.

"He wants our nephew." The uncle sounded mildly surprised, and tired beyond discussion. He averted his eyes, deferring to his wife.

"This boy?!" The aunt grabbed him by the ear and dragged him out from behind his protector. She could see from his manner that he had sold no wood. She looked as if she would strike him, but then her posture changed. Her eyes narrowed shrewdly, and she looked from the boy to the man. "It will cost us to lose him. Who will bring our wood and water? Besides, he was my husband's brother's son, and we have loved him like our own. You must pay us a bag of gold for him."

A silence fell. The uncle shifted uncomfortably. The mage held the eyes of the aunt, his expression unreadable. "I will give you a bag of gold," he answered finally, "for he is worth that and more to me. You will see in the morning, when you look at the coins, that you have been paid fairly; the value you have placed on your nephew will be there in the bag."

The aunt took the bag and weighed it in her hand. She opened it immediately. Gold gleamed in the firelight. Satisfied, she tied the bag shut and stuffed it into her dress. "Be gone with him, then," she said.

The mage and the boy took their leave. Outside, the mage stopped. As promised, he bent and drew a rune on the doorstep with his finger. As the boy watched, it shimmered in the darkness and then was gone. "How do you know what to write?" the boy asked, suddenly anxious. "What if it tells him to go to the wrong place?"

"It doesn't tell him where to go. Your bond does that. You call him to yourself, as you have been calling ever since he left. The rune just lets him hear you more clearly, so he can follow."

The boy bent to touch the ground. Just then the door swung open. The aunt stood silhouetted by the hearth fire. "What are you doing here still?" she demanded.

"We are leaving," said the mage evenly, and she slammed the door.

The boy looked up, apologetically. "You shouldn't have paid her gold for me," he said. "She didn't love me. She would have given me away for free."

"She has been paid fairly," said the mage. "You and I may both be wrong, but I would be surprised if, when she wakes in the morning, that bag contains more than a few coppers."

The mage set off through the street, and the boy fell in behind him, buffered from the blowing snow by the body of the man and hugging to himself the warmth of the flame.

They stayed that night in a barn. The boy collapsed in the hay against the warm back of a sleeping calf and thought it the most comfortable bed he had ever known. The next evening they arrived at the junction of two roads and a river, at an inn built of tumbled rocks and stout timbers. "Tomorrow we turn toward the sea," said the mage. "In two days we will be home." *Home*, repeated the boy to himself. He marveled at the thought of it.

"Welcome back, sir," said the innkeeper. He was a short man, as solid looking as the inn itself, his arms laden with large mugs of ale and bowls of stew. He gestured to a table near a wide fireplace and then moved off to deliver the food he was holding.

The mage slipped out of his pack and made himself comfortable. The boy slid into a chair with his back to the wall and sat wide-eyed, absorbing the hum of conversation, the solid expanse of the room, and the curious clothes and manners of the travelers. He realized abruptly that the mage was talking to him, pointing out the dinner that sat on the table in front of them. He flushed and apologized. The man laughed. "Take it all in," he said. "The more you know the world around you, the better you will know yourself."

After dinner, as they sat by the fire, the innkeeper's wife approached them. She ducked her head awkwardly and twisted her apron. "My Arnie's ailing, sir …," she fumbled for words, red faced.

"Of course," said the mage, and, rising to follow her, he beckoned the boy.

Arnie was a child with an odd face, a twisted back and a withered arm, who lay in a wide family bed, wheezing and coughing in fitful sleep. The man laid a hand on the child's forehead and listened for a while. "Is it the fever?" asked the anxious mother, breaking the silence.

"No," said the mage. "A lesser illness. Make a tent over the bed and inside it put a pan of boiling water, so deep." He showed her with his hands. Then he drew a cloth bag out of a pocket and handed her some dried leaves. "Add these, then drop in stones from the fire." Then he turned back to the sick child, touching him again, murmuring words that the boy did not understand. The mother clutched the dried leaves as if they were gold. She stumbled over words of appreciation as she had stumbled over her request.

After they left the room, the man turned to the boy. "What is the most important question in your mind right now?" he asked.

"What was in that …" The boy stopped. *The most important question*. He tried again. "How do you know what to do?" he asked.

"Is that the most important question?" responded the man.

The boy hesitated. "No," he said softly with discomfort. The man waited. "Why?" The boy stammered. "Why bother? What is the point of saving a child like that? My uncle's lambs …" He flushed.

"Yes," said the man, nodding. "That is the most important question. 'Why' usually will be the most important question. It also is the one you must answer for yourself; neither I nor anyone else can answer it for you.

"Tonight, though, I will tell you how I answered for *my*self: The mother loves him."

"But the child can't do anything … He doesn't look right, I mean he looks like he can't think right."

"You are correct," said the man. "He can't think any better than he can walk. But the mother loves him. She loves this child regardless of his ability to walk or to think. She loves him without consideration for what other children can or cannot do. And I would rather live in a world that contains her love than one that contains her grief. This is why I help her."

The boy frowned, bothered though he couldn't explain why. "I don't see how he deserves it."

"Love is a gift. It is not earned, though it can be destroyed, either willfully or carelessly. It is always undeserved. It is apart from deserving, beyond deserving."

"It must be amazing to be loved like that," said the boy wistfully, thinking of his own mother, whose image was more and more difficult to draw into memory

"Do you think you are not," asked the man in reproof, "when your brother's love could send me through the dark forests in winter?"

"Oh," the boy gasped. He flushed, ashamed. He hadn't known he was envious until the envy disappeared. In its place swelled a feeling of being loved enormously.

"Now," said the man, smiling. "Would you still like to know what was in the bag?"

In the early summer, a lanky young man with a rough bundle on his back arrived at the gates of a coastal town. Following a hunch he could not exactly explain, he made his way through the streets toward the central square and back out again from the center. He turned onto a cobbled alley, and a boy stepped out of a doorway, scanned the street as if he had been called, and began to run. The boy flung himself on the young man, who, journey-weary, staggered backward before catching his balance and wrapping his arms around the brother who had knocked his breath away. They held each other in the timeless embrace of those who have been apart too long, and then walked hand in hand to the open door.

The Tree

There was a time when the coastal plains stood dark and heavy with ancient trees, and farms lay scattered like emeralds along twisted silver threads of stream and river. The air hung thick with the smells of life and of death and the sense of mysterious powers that were neither. In those days a widow lived in a glen, bounded on one side by a river that flowed from the mountains to the western sea, and on the other by the road that ran from the steppe to the southlands.

She lived with her only child, a daughter. Together they tended a garden of herbs and vegetables and summer fruits, and together they kept a flock of goats. When the sun shone bright, they would wave to their neighbors on the far side of the river, but seldom did they cross the ford, save for the festivals of rebirth and harvest. On those days, a market of tents appeared upriver and the people of the nearest farms made their way along the forest paths to join together in six days of selling and buying and feasting and dancing. Mostly, they traded with travelers and wanderers who passed on the road. Not infrequently, when the shadows fell, they fed a weary guest and laid a mat by the fire and listened to tales of far-off lands. This was their tie to the world of humans.

The daughter was long-legged and strong, and the seasonal rhythm of hoeing and harvesting, milking and shearing came naturally to her. But as she listened to the stories of travelers and the visions of pilgrims, a dream began to grow. She longed to see monuments and holy places and the Great Library, to seek the knowledge of philosophers and the wisdom of the wise. She wanted to live among the seekers in the cloisters of the Eyrie and study the power of the ancients. But she dreamed this dream in silence on her knees in the milking shed, or on a ladder in the orchard, for she could not leave her mother to tend the farm alone.

In the third spring of the daughter's womanhood, they were joined by the widow's brother, who had been a cobbler in the city of the king. "My wife has gone the way of her father," he said, "and I have left the shop to my sons. I am not needed, and I find there no peace." Loss hung havey on him; sadness wrapped around him like a blanket. But as he joined in the simple labors of the season, planting and pruning and birthing, his grief thinned and faxed, and he lifted his face one more to the sun. He settled and stayed, sending word to his sons that he had taken root.

Secure, then, in the confidence that her mother had a companion and partner in the labors of the farm, the daughter confessed her dream one evening by the fireside. By then it had become a determination. Her mother wept, but made no move to dissuade her. "I have known," she said. "I have known you needed to go."

So when the harvest was preserved in the rafters and the pantry, and the barn and roof were winter-tight, after the festival had come and gone, they bound clothing and food in her pack and stitched coins in her hem. The daughter tied her knife at her waist, wrapped herself in a woolen cloak, and bid her mother and uncle goodbye. She left in the company of pilgrims returning from the steppe. Deep in a pocket, she carried a message on parchment from her uncle, an introduction to an elder he had known in his years in the Royal City.

The widow walked with her daughter to the path for a final embrace. She watched as the small traveling party cross the ford and continued out of sight into the forest. Then she returned home to the comfort of the necessary: animals that needed feeding, water that needed to be carried from the river, dishes that needed washing. Thoughts of her daughter filled her as she worked. In her mind's eye, she followed her daughter through the forest, over stones, around rutted mud, under overhanging trees that obscured the sun, through clearings were bright finches hunted seeds of thistle and poppy and formations of geese passed overhead, following the sun south.

She awoke the next morning aching with absence. After she finished her early chores, her brother working in respectful silence at her side, the widow made her way back to the place she had last seen her daughter, tall and sure, bundle strapped to her back. There, not far from where the path met the river, stood a tree that she held sacred. It stood alone, apart from the forest edge: an oak, with a trunk as massive to her as her father had been when she scarcely reached his knee.

Its branches reached toward the forest, toward the river, toward the path, toward the house. She leaned against the trunk and looked up at the stark black tangle, dizzying in its immensity, linking each direction to all and drawing them together into the vastness of the sky. "Here," she said aloud to her daughter, "here we are together. Here my spirit calls to your spirit and I touch you."

She then took from her head a bright woven scarf and tied it on a low branch of the tree, anchoring her presence to that place. Afterward, the widow came to the tree often, speaking her love to her daughter, singing her love, crying her love … and envisioning her daughter through the seasons of sun, wind, rain, and snow.

In the spring a pilgrim on the road noticed the mother's scarf. The bright flutter caught his eye. He hesitated, then approached the tree. *It is a message*, he thought. *This is a place of message.* And then, with wonder, he saw the tree as the widow saw it. He knelt, lost to time, and with his spirit, spoke to people he loved in far off places. At last he stood, stiff and awkward. He reached into his pocket and drew out a soft, worn, cotton cloth. He carefully removed the coins it contained, replaced them in his pocket, and tied the piece of frayed white cotton to wave beside the scarf.

Not long after, a merchant stopped. He held up his hand. His indentured boy brought the laden mules to a halt, then stood waiting with the line of animals, wet from the ford. The merchant approached the tree, now green with life, and touched its bark as one might touch the robe of a sage or a healer. Long he stood with his face lifted toward the leafy canopy. Then he returned to the mules. Patiently he worked the knots on one of the bundles until an oblong canvas bag came free and fell to the ground. From it, he drew out a bolt of silk, purple and gold, woven with the plants and birds of an artist's vision. Returning to the tree, he wound the silk around the trunk, tying it tight but leaving the ends to flow with the breath of the spring air.

"What are you doing?" asked the boy, when the man returned to the mules. The silk was worth more than his year's wages. "I am telling my wife I love her," the man answered. "I am sending her strength and hope." The man turned away, his eyes filled with secret tears, for his wife lay ill in their distant home. The boy shook his head, dismayed and bewildered, leaving the silk behind reluctantly when the man prodded the mules again toward the path before them.

But the widow understood, when she returned to the tree the following day. She touched the silk with a smile of recognition. She closed her eyes, and it seemed to her that the movement of the silk and cotton merged with that of her own wool scarf, harmonizing and amplifying the message she sent forth to her daughter.

Throughout that summer, many stopped: Now a wanderer. Now a band of performers heading for the cities of the north. Now a traveling blacksmith, bearing the utensils and pots he had made at his winter forge and the tools he needed for repairing broken farm implements. Each, coming to the tree, saw something that made them hesitate and draw near. Each felt something that drew from them their whispered yearnings and gave them hope to say what needed saying, confident somehow that their messages of love would be heard. And each left behind an object, a token of their presence in that place.

Years passed. Rumors drifted north and south, of a tree along the old road, a place of power on the forested plain. Then more people came, not passing peddlers or those with a wanderlust, but people seeking the wonder of the tree. And when they arrived, they found the tree bound in ribbons of cloth, some tattered and faded, some bright and new. Folded parchments protruded from cracks in the bark and under the roots. Smooth stones, oil-rubbed and marked with coal, lay scattered on the ground. One year a cairn appeared, built laboriously of river rocks, to stand beside the tree. On it lay a carving of a human hand, palm open to the sky.

A later year brought a train of mules, dragging long planks that were reassembled into a wooden platform for kneeling. The platform was made of teak and carved with dragons, and it arrived worn and darkened from the touch of many hands. The widow smiled her knowing smile when she approached it. She had seen an encampment for several days by the tree and had stayed away. Now the visitors were gone, leaving behind only this wooden structure. She stooped and traced newly carved words with her fingertips:

For strength drawn from the earth and borne on the wind.
For life beyond hope.
For peace beyond life.

She removed her shoes and stepped onto the platform, then knelt, bending slowly, for her knees and back had stiffened with age. She closed her eyes, and with her mind's eye followed her daughter as she had for so many seasons. She had seen her in the cobbled streets of the Royal City, knocking at the elder's door and being received. She had seen her carrying water and grinding herbs under the eye of a watchful tutor. She had seen her standing before the gates of the Great Library, and bent over ancient manuscripts. She had seen her in the towers of the Eyrie, chanting in a gray robe and kneeling by a sick child. Now she saw her in the chambers of the Council. "For strength drawn from the earth and borne on the wind," she whispered.

The widow and her brother grew old together. The house had grown too, for the brother had been followed by his grandson, who arrived from the city with a wife and young children. The labor of the elders gradually diminished. The older woman found herself less and less chasing goats and more and more peeling vegetables and wiping faces and knitting on the new porch – "new" though it had stood for more than ten years by the time she finally handed off the goats altogether. "I can make cheese and knit goat wool into sweaters and scarves," she said. "But if I have to chase down those nannies for milking and shearing we will all go hungry and cold."

One day a messenger arrived with a folded parchment. It was sealed with wax. Inside was a letter from the daughter, saying she would arrive for a visit before the apples turned ripe for harvest. At the widow's request, the messenger read it aloud.

"Are you her mother?" he asked in a tone of awe. "Are you the mother of she whose counsel is sought by the seekers?" He made a gesture of respect.

"We are all children of the one Mother," answered the widow. She dipped a cup of cool water from the earthen vessel by the door and held it out to him. "Drink," she said laughing. "Drink of our Mother's milk."

When the messenger had gone, the widow carried the parchment to the tree. She placed it carefully in a hollow near the base, then, leaning against the trunk, looked up at the familiar limbs and the vast green of the summer canopy. "I have known," she said. "I have known you needed to come home."

The daughter arrived, as promised, in the early fall. She crossed the ford, followed by two students, a mule bearing gifts, and a tall daughter of her own. She stopped, as had so many, compelled by the majestic form that rose before her. Shoes in hand, she walked toward the tree, marveling at the movement of fabric and paper. She touched the rock sculpture, the wooden platform, and lastly the tree itself. Then she sank to her knees with a gasp of laughter and tears. "Look," she called to her students and her daughter. "Come. Look. I have spent my life in search of the spirit that is here."

From across the field, a woman hurried toward them, small with age, stumbling over the stick that supported part of her weight, yet bright with the anticipation of joy.

The Peddler

Once there was a village in a faraway country beyond the mountains. The people of the village lived in peace until there came, one day, a peddler with three laden donkeys. The first carried shimmering silks, woven in the colors of the sunset and wildflowers and butterfly wings. Wrapped inside the silks were mirrors of polished silver, with twining vines or branches curving around their handles, the backs decorated with meadows and grasslands and forests, in bright enamel, set with many-colored jewels. The second donkey packed knives and swords, as polished as the mirrors, etched with scenes of great battles and fortresses, and equally remarkable tools. The third supported boxes made of stone.

"Come," the peddler called to the villagers. "Buy my wares. Are they not enchanting?" To the women he said, "Wear my silks and you shall become more beautiful than all the earth, for the colors of the earth will be yours and only yours, and the rich sensuality of the earth will be yours alone. You will be desired, you will be needed, for only in you will others experience supreme beauty."

To the men he said, "Buy my weapons and my tools, and you shall become stronger than nature. The strength of the mountains, the strength of the cities of men, the strength of great builders past and present will be yours. You will be respected, you will be honored, you will have the power to implement your dreams, for none will stand before you."

The people came. The women saw truly that the fabrics were more beautiful than any they had ever seen. They looked at their own clothing of homespun wool and cotton with simple embroideries, and they felt ashamed. They looked at each other fingering the silks, which shimmered softly in the afternoon light. Each thought of the others … *they will buy and I alone will be left dull and gray.*

The men saw truly that the knives and swords and tools were of finest quality, forged with a heat and precision beyond their capability, and of unfamiliar metals. "From the heart of the earth," the peddler said. They hefted them, they swung them teasingly at each other. But mostly each watched carefully as his fellows tested the peddler's weapons. They thought of their own rough implements, beaten over a simple forge, cast with painstaking labor in vessels made of wax and clay, and they felt ashamed. Each thought of the others … *they will buy and I alone will be left weak.*

"What is the price?" they asked the peddler. "What do you ask for your wares?"

"Very little," he replied. "Something you won't even miss. All I ask is that you give me in trade your other beauty and your other strength."

The villagers looked at each other then, believing him mad. "Take them if you can," they laughed, thinking he could not. "Anyhow, what need have we of other beauty and strength when all that exists in the world will be ours."

Each chose what he or she would claim. Then the peddler unpacked the donkey with the boxes made of stone. He opened them and handed one to each of the villagers. "Put your beauty and strength in here," he said. The people could barely contain their laughter. Thinking he was a fool or a madman, they humored him, each pretending to put something in the box, then closing it and handing it back. The peddler gathered them up, bundled them together, and left. Then there was much merriment, for the people believed that they had gotten the best bargain of their lives – something for nothing – and they carried home their new possessions.

But they were wrong.

The goods were indeed enchanting and served as the peddler had promised. The men were indomitable, commanding all others to do as they desired and to create whatever they desired. The women were beautiful beyond compare, commanding all hearts to do their bidding.

Then the people started to leave their village, becoming powerful throughout the land, drawing all to themselves through awe and desire and fear. They seduced their way through the gates of walled cities and took control. They broke the barricades of those who resisted. They channeled labor, at a great cost in human suffering, into monuments that glorified their bodies and their dominance. In time, their descendants ruled the world.

But power was all they had.

The earth itself faded before the beauty of the women, because the magician (for that is what he was) had truly stolen the colors from the butterflies and flowers and sunset. Earthquakes and avalanches increased, for the magician had truly plundered the metals from the heart of the earth. The land they ruled was broken, void of the stolen colors, shaken by the tremors of the earth. The people they ruled also were broken. They were bereft of the glories of nature, save in their rulers, and they languished, for they could not work hard enough to fulfill the endless demands of those in power and still meet their own needs.

Eventually, even the rulers themselves were unhappy, for the magician had carried away in his stone boxes their strength and beauty of character and community. The jealousy that had been aroused when first they saw the silks and weapons filled the emptiness left by that which they had given up. The men began to wage fierce battles among themselves, competing for territory and control belonging to another. The women maneuvered and manipulated, each vying for any heart that might have been given to another. And yet, as promised, none missed what they had forfeited.

Many years passed this way. The silks and weapons, which seemed indestructible, were handed from one generation to the next, each becoming more powerful than the one that came before. But the people who were enslaved did not forget how it once had been. From parent to child, the stories passed of a different time and another kind of world.

One day, a young goatherd girl was searching for a stray goat that had wandered from her flock. She lived in the mountains near the very village where the magician had sold his wares so long ago. She got lost. She didn't come home that night, and in the morning her mother and brother closed up their house and set out to look for her. Her father was away in the valley, as he must be for three months every year, working at the towering fortress that guarded their rulers.

"She is this way," the mother said, "I have a sense of it." So they set off through the forest, crossing familiar land and then unfamiliar, climbing higher and higher up a tangled river valley, until, as the sun began to sink, they emerged upon the ruin of an abandoned village and found the girl, sitting in a grassy square among the ruins, strangely still.

They approached the girl, knelt beside her and touched her, and she shook herself, as if from a trance. "Look," she said, pointing to the sky. "The light is different here." And so it was. The sunset flowed magenta and gold above the valley, casting shadows of deep purple and blue. Bright red poppies peeked out on slender stems from between the paving stones of the square. The stone ruins rose up, in all variants of brown, from limestone to brick to darkest velvet. Water shone iridescent, first silver then turquoise, in the basin of an old fountain. The mother and brother, struck silent by the natural beauty of this place, slowly sat down beside her.

Suddenly, an old man in a rainbow colored cloak appeared from behind one of the stone pillars. "You didn't think I would sell it all and not save enough for myself, did you?" The three remained silent, staring at the wrinkled figure and his brilliantly colored wrap, wondering who he was and whether they had somehow left their own world for another.

"You too can have these colors," said the shriveled face. He reached into a pocket of his cape and pulled out objects that could not have fit there: silken scarves woven with the same vibrant hues as the sunset, mirrors that reflected the rich red poppies and velvety brown ruins, polished knives that glistened and gleamed like the water in the old fountain. He held these treasures out in front of them.

The young girl started to reach for a scarf, but the mother stayed her hand. The boy shifted toward one of the knives, but his sister touched his shoulder. "What is the price?" asked the mother.

"Very little," said the figure before them. "Something you won't even miss." Then he reached into his cloak with his other hand and presented them with three small stone boxes.

The three sat gazing upon the beauty they had been craving all their lives without knowing it, and at the power to fight back against the tyranny that kept their husband and father a slave through three long months a year, draining his life energy and their own. But they did not laugh at his price; they weighed it.

"No," said the mother at last. "My children are more beautiful than even the colors around us. And I am stronger than you know. What you ask I will not give."

The magician looked at the children. "You can choose for yourselves," he said. "You don't need to abide by your mother's decision. Don't listen to her. Look at what I offer. Have you ever seen anything like it? You never will again."

"No," said the brother, slowly, regretfully. "Our mother is beautiful in ways that you cannot imagine."

"And," added the girl, recalling a liturgy they had been taught years before, "We are as strong as the earth herself, who bore us all."

"You are fools," said the magician. "You could have had unlimited beauty and power." But he was lying.

The three departed and walked down the mountainside together. The deep creases in the mother's face began to soften, as she left behind the fatigue that comes after two days of worry. The evening chill made the children shiver, but they held hands and stumbled playfully against each other through the darkening forest. And gold and purple streaks lingered in the sky above them as they approached their village.

When at last they arrived at their cottage and the mother lit a candle, the children noticed that her dress was nearly as red as the poppies they had seen at the ruins. The mother saw that the bread she cut for her children was rich and brown. And a vivid green stem of honeysuckle, barely visible before, twined peacefully through their window.

The Calling

In the southern wilderness, on the rocky coast, a small family lived in a cottage made of cedar planks. In front, the cottage faced the western sea, gray and rough through the long months of winter when the wind beat rain against the windows and sent gusts of cold salt air down the chimney if the fire was low. In summer, the water lay calm and beckoning, and the light of the setting sun silhouetted black islands on the horizon.

Behind the cottage lay a small farm, just a goat pen and a clearing carved out of a forest of immense trees whose limbs of deep feathery green stretched above trunks wrapped in soft red paper bark. A vegetable garden and a pair of plum trees wrestled against the wilderness and the goats.

The family consisted of a mother and a daughter. The mother worked making nets for the fishermen of a settlement not far to the north of the cottage. All summer she gathered bark, moving through the forest with a basket on her back, pulling long vertical strips from the trees. These she soaked in a solution that softened them further, so that the long months of winter could be spent pounding and weaving and splicing and knotting.

The daughter did what she could to help. From the time she learned to walk, she accompanied her mother into the forest, carrying a small pail, gathering flowers that she would tuck into the crevices of the cabin in the spring, picking berries that grew at the edge of the clearings in the late summer and early fall, collecting (with her mother's direction) herbs for tea or mushrooms for soup as these came into season. She would stroke her mother's tired sore hands when they stopped in a glade for lunch and would sing the eerie meandering folk songs that had been sung to her in her cradle.

"Tell me the story of my father," she often would say if her mother had the energy for conversation. The mother would smile a knowing smile at this little daughter who never tired of the telling. She would touch her daughter's cheek or tuck away a wisp of hair or pull the small body into her lap, and then she would begin a well-worn story in which every word was as familiar to them as the knots in the cabin floor or the steamy scents of the summer meadow or the sound of waves on the stony shore.

"When I was young," she would begin, "and I slept in the house of my mother and my hair hung free, I lived in a town to the north of here. My feet were nimble and my hands were quick. I could weave a fine woolen scarf and bake a loaf of soft brown bread and dance the fourteen parts of the Spring Awakening. I thought I had learned all I needed to know and I was impatient to be a woman. So when I carried water from the well I studied the men I passed in the square and the streets, the shepherds and boat builders, the blacksmiths, goldsmiths and cabinet makers, the farmers and the merchants, until I saw one that caught my eye. He was a stout lad, a carpenter, with soft dark curls and eyes the color of the winter sea."

"Was he my father?" asked the child, knowing the answer.

"No," said the mother, "though I was unwavering in my choice and married him sooner than my parents might have wished. He loved his drink more than he could ever love me, and though I lived five years in his mother's house, it was clear that we would never have a home of our own, for his time and earnings went to the pub. His mother was harsh; I served not only her, but her sister and aunt as well. It was an unhappy place, and I would bring no child to live there, choosing instead the herbs that close the womb."

The child nodded, knowing neither which herbs these might be nor the meaning of the word "womb" but relishing the familiar phrases.

"One day he left with a merchant friend for the pubs of the Royal City, and he never returned. At the end of the One Year's Waiting, I was free and returned to my mother's hearth. With wisdom gleaned from my experience of having bound myself to a sodden husband and bitter mother-in-law, I relished the comfort of my childhood home, joining my mother in her weaving and helping my father tend his shoe repair for nine years as his health declined. My father and then my mother, grown weary with age, entered the houses of their fathers, and I was alone."

"I wish *I* had been there," said the child, fiercely. "Then you wouldn't have been alone."

The mother smiled at her insistent protectiveness. "At the Spring Awakening that followed the sending of my mother, I stood in the crowd and watched the young girls dance. I thought of the time I had lost and I wished for a child. When I looked up, a man was watching me, a tall man with green eyes and hair the color of bark soaking in the sun."

"Like my hair?" asked the daughter.

"Like yours," said the mother.

"Like my eyes?" asked the daughter.

"Like yours," said the mother.

"Ah," sighed the child contentedly.

"When the dancing ended, he followed me home and I took him to my bed."

"To make a child," commented the girl, knowing.

"To make a child. He stayed for two months, and then he left, back to his ship which sailed for the west. But those months were the happiest of my life, save maybe the time that I first looked into your eyes, little one. We lay on the rooftop and let the morning sun bathe our faces. We sipped tea by the hearth. We swam in the wide lazy turns of the river above the town. We sat on a bench in the port and watched men, like ants in a line, carrying boxes and trunks and great odd packages down the planks. I closed the shoe repair and took no customers, relishing only the delights of his companionship and my own senses. Then he left."

"You should have gone with him!"

"You know why I did not. I spoke not his language; he spoke not mine. His home lay in the west, far across the sea. His boat was laden with timber and salted fish, not lonely women or household goods. I waved goodbye from the dock, lightly as if I did not care about his leaving."

"But you did care, didn't you?"

"Yes, I cared."

"And then what?"

"And then I went home, and a little child started growing in me. I worked in the shop until one day, when you were big in my belly, the landlord came to me. He was a haughty man who had inherited the properties on which the house and shop stood. 'I think it is time for you to move on,' he said. He looked around the tools and he looked at my shape. 'I do not think you will be able to pay the rent next month.' 'But I *have* paid the rent,' I said, 'I am working to pay the rent now. I will do the same with a child.' 'Perhaps,' he said in a cold voice, 'But that was the old rent, the rent my father agreed upon with your father. I think next month you will find things quite different.' He told me the new price, and I saw that he wanted me out. Perhaps he thought to find another kind of business that could pay him more. Perhaps he did not like the idea of a woman repairing shoes. Perhaps he thought that once you were born it would be harder to force me to leave.

"I was worried but mostly angry. I searched the town but could find no way to earn what I needed without submitting again to a mistress, which I had vowed never to do.

I will find a place that is different, I told myself, where I can take care of myself and my child and where no one can tell me what to cook or when to leave. The neighbors advised me differently, but I sold all I had and joined a group of pilgrims heading south. So it was that I came here, with you in my belly and a bundle on my back, and a small bag of coins.

"A kind family in the village, the cousins of my father's uncle, took me in for the weeks before your birth. From them I learned of this place; the elderly owners had recently joined their fathers, and the heirs wanted nothing of it. They traded the house and the furnishings and the tools and even the goats for my bag of coins, though I think they might have gotten much more if they were less impatient. And here we are."

"But there was something you didn't sell," prompted the child.

"Yes," said the mother. "Before your father left, he took a chain from around his neck. From it hung a medallion with a golden lion looking outward, as if the lion could see the world. Your father touched my belly and placed the medallion around my neck."

"For me," sighed the child. "He meant it for me. He knew I was coming."

"For you," the mother agreed.

"What was his name?"

The mother told her, as she had before, and the child sang the name to herself. As she grew, she sang her father's name as she played and she sang it as she helped her mother at the spindle or at the hearth, and she sang it soundlessly as she drifted off to sleep. She imagined her father, lean and strong, the owner or the captain or the first mate of the ship that had brought him to their shore. She imagined him a nobleman in his home country, directing servants and riding sleek horses. She imagined him thinking of his child, far away, wondering about her, wishing to know her. She imagined finding him and bringing him home to her weary mother, and seeing again the joy of those two months.

As the years passed, their lives changed little. In the summer of the daughter's eleventh year, they were joined on the farm by the mother's distant cousin, a strong middle-aged widow whose grown sons worked on merchant ships and could offer her no home. She brought a trunk of warm quilts, her spinning wheel and loom, and bulbs she had tended in pots each spring since she was a young bride. And the cousin brought four precious books, which she taught the girl to read.

I must know how to read when I find my father, the girl told herself. She labored over the pages, in the name of her dream. The books opened her to other dreams: healers in their shops of drying herbs, artists creating windows of rainbow light, and sages in the great halls of learning in the Royal City. But she paid little attention to these, for the only story that compelled her was the one of her heritage.

The cousin also taught her numbers, the tricks of tallying and tracking and adding used by the shopkeepers. *I will know how to add when I find my father*, the girl promised herself, and she worked hard on the learning. She kept ledgers of bark gathered and nets woven and potatoes harvested, which she wrote on scraps of bark using a sharpened bit of coal.

This learning opened to her possibilities of employment in the fishing village. In the summer she took work in a dry goods store, tending the till while the mistress tended her newborn. On the way home she would walk along the water's edge. She carried home her pay in coppers and wheat flour and remnants of cloth. When the sun was low, her eyes followed the birds that flew westward to the islands at the water's edge. She pretended that those dark silhouettes were her father's home, that he lived just beyond the meeting of sky and sea, and that she was on her way to meet him, sailing in a small boat with silken sails. She wore the medallion that her mother had given her at her coming of age, and she held it up so that it caught the sun and flashed on the water, signaling her presence to the far off horizon.

Sometimes when she got home, she would ask her mother for the old story and ply her for details of the father's look and manner. Once, when her mother was too tired to respond, the girl made her a cup of tea and told the story herself, word for word.

"Why do you keep asking when you know every detail?" asked the surprised cousin.

"Because it is my story. Because I need to know who I am," said the girl.

"No," said the cousin. "It is your mother's story, and part of your father's. You are not who you come from. To know who you are takes a different kind of asking." The girl scowled at the intrusion and offered her mother another cup of tea.

When she turned seventeen, she said to her mother, "I am going to find my father."

The mother tried to dissuade her, but she saw that her daughter was as unwavering as she herself had been in her youth. So she made arrangements for the daughter to travel north in the company of a merchant's pack train to the town of her beginnings. With the help of the quietly disapproving cousin, the mother penned a note asking hospitality from distant relatives. She selected the best of their dried cheeses and brought out a knotted cloth that contained all the coins she had hoarded over her years of weaving.

These she sewed into a small pack for her daughter, along with a thick wool blanket. "Go with my blessing," she said, though her heart ached with the fear that she would never see her child again. She saved her tears for the solitude that followed.

The daughter was welcomed into the home of her mother's relations, and the young woman, whose hands had been busy since childhood, quickly filled her time. With the skills she had acquired, she made herself useful in her relatives' apothecary shop, as she began to learn the trade. She offered to help their children with letters and numbers, and before long, she was spending her evenings surrounded by a small gathering of bent heads and scratching slates.

The sights and sounds of the town were curious and wonderful to her. One day, her relatives took her to the harbormaster, who, by searching an archive of yellowed ledgers, was able to tell her the port of origin of her father's ship. She then found an elderly woman who had grown up in the western city where her father's ship originated. From her, the daughter memorized what the old woman remembered of her childhood tongue. *When I see my father, I will be able to speak with him*, she promised herself. Then she waited, hoping a ship would come again from the city of her father.

Months stretched into a year and then longer. Trade patterns shifted and no ships came from the west. Twice since she arrived, she had sent letters home to her mother (and twice in the following months she had received a response). Now she sent another. "Do not write to me again in this place; I leave next week for the Royal City. No western ships have come, and though I wait another year it may be that none are coming. I am told that ships from the west are received now at the Royal City, where the water is deeper and the port more sheltered. I am determined, and I will find what I seek."

The trip to the Royal City was longer and harder than the fortnight of walking it had taken to reach the town of her relations. It was spring and rainy, and the road was rutted and deep with mud. But when she arrived, she found what she was looking for. A ship's captain who had married a foreigner intended to take his wife and children on the westward voyage. He would trade her berth for tutoring.

In the weeks before the departure, the young woman discovered the library of her people, protected by guardian monks, but free to all who sought knowledge there. For the first time, she realized the many doors open to her due to her literacy. Her recent experience in the apothecary shop drew her to the tomes about disease and injury and the healing arts. She remembered the scars and crippling she had seen in the fishing village of her youth, and she was astonished by the knowledge contained in these volumes, information that would have made such damage avoidable. When the time came for her ship to set sail, she left the books reluctantly. "Have you found a calling?" asked the monk who opened the tall door for her departure. The question echoed as she walked down a narrow cobbled alley, through a busy market, and arrived at the port, where she retrieved her few possessions in a small let room and headed for the ship.

The time at sea was a delight to the young woman. The ship sailed between islands of the same chain she had seen from the windows of her mother's cottage and rocky beach. Her childhood fantasies melted into awed appreciation of the windswept cliffs and gnarled vegetation. Then came a vast emptiness of sky and sea that reached beyond the curve of the horizon. This void seemed to magically propel the ship onward, until they arrived at last in the port of a city, silhouetted by dark spires with green copper roofs. As the ship drew closer, she gasped – atop the arched gateway guarding the port stood great carved lions.

In response to this vision, the young woman touched the golden lion that hung beneath her clothing and felt her heart pounding with hope. She quickly took her leave of the ship and her traveling companions. "You are welcome to return with us when we depart," said the captain. "You are a good teacher and my children have loved your company. We will leave by midmonth." The young woman thanked him, but her mind was elsewhere.

As she passed between the lions of the gateway, she entered a square filled with a bustle of people and vendors' stalls. Ahead of her, against a gnarled tree trunk, sat a shabby booth with a veil-wrapped woman inside. Over the booth hung a small sign containing a message written in three languages:

Professional Finder
What Do You Seek?

Though she was skeptical of "finding" rituals (similar practitioners advertised in her homeland), she crossed the street and approached the booth. Her time felt short, and she was daunted by the immensity of the city and the country in which it lay. Yet, she was compelled to speak to the finder.

When she stopped in front of the booth, the veiled woman spoke, uncovering her face as she did so. Gray hair lay bound and matted above a dark wrinkled face, with eyes of pale watery blue. "What is your search?" she asked in the foreign tongue. "In order for me to help you, I must know what you seek . . . and why."

"And why?" faltered the young woman.

"Yes," said the finder. "The soul of your quest. The substance of finding lies not in *what* but in *why*. But first I must see your coins."

The young woman hesitated, but showed her the coins, wondering if the finder would try to demand them all. But the old woman withdrew only two coppers and then sat waiting and watching.

Stumbling over the little-used language, the young woman explained why she had come. She spoke of her mother and of her childhood dream. She spoke the name of her father and showed the medallion on which the golden lion looked back at the finder with a gaze that rivaled that of the wizened woman.

The finder looked at the lion for a long time. Then she stared up at the lions that stood across the square. She closed her eyes in silent meditation, and then finally she spoke.

"With regard to your first goal," she said, "do not be so sure that your mother is unhappy with the life she has chosen, though it may be hard. She did not choose the path she is on once but many times. Each of us must weigh alone which doors to pass through and which to pass by." She was silent again for several minutes.

"And with regard to your second." Now she fixed the young woman with her penetrating gaze. "If he is a sage or a beggar, will you know who you are? If he is a nobleman, will you know? If he beats his slaves, if he makes spires that reach heavenward or weapons of war, if pilgrims travel across the mountains to touch the hem of his cloak, will you know?" The girl did not answer. She looked down at her feet and tears of frustration welled in her eyes.

The old woman spoke one last time. "Your father's name is well known in this town," she said, and she gave directions to his residence.

Shortly thereafter, the young woman stared up at the heavily curtained windows of a three-story stone residence which pressed on either side against homes that were narrower and less ornate. Carts and people came and went, but she paid them no notice. Her reverie was interrupted, though, by a shriek and a crash. A young boy carrying a heavy earthen jug had gotten jostled into the side of an oxcart. He lost his balance and fell, smashing the jug and catching his fingers under the edge of the rough, iron-bound wheel. He landed nearly at her feet.

The young woman bent to help, while others, seeing that the boy had care, let her be. Surprised by her insistent ministrations and her curious, halting speech, the boy quieted and allowed her to wash his injured hand with water that trickled from a nearby public spigot. He watched as she dug in her pack for herbs to staunch bleeding and to ease pain (a parting gift from her relations in the apothecary shop). And when she tucked a copper coin into his uninjured hand, the boy looked at her wide-eyed, wiped his nose on his sleeve, gave an odd little bow, and ran for home.

The young woman stood up and reset her pack on her back. *What am I doing here?*, she said to herself. *I know who I am!*

She walked across the street and touched a grating on one of the lower windows of the residence, as if to say goodbye. As she turned to go, the door opened and a man in a cloak came down the marble steps. He was a tall man, with green eyes and hair the color of cedar soaking in water, scattered with gray at the temples and crown. He stopped, waiting for a horse carriage that approached from the far end of the block. The young woman in foreign clothes caught his eye. He studied her with a slight frown, and she met his gaze. "Can I help you?" he asked.

"No, you cannot," she replied with a small laugh. "But please allow me to introduce myself."

The Message

In an ancient seaside town, off of a dark alley too narrow for carts, a girl lived with her widowed mother. They lived in a single room with no window to enjoy the seascape, just a sagging plank door that scraped the stone threshold whenever it was opened or closed. The mother took in mending, spending her days in a chair in the doorway, bent over a darning bob and an old sock, or a needle and an open seam, or a patch fitted carefully to yet another pair of trousers with gaping knees.

The clothes she mended were worn, often threadbare, for times were hard, and the neighbors had little more than the woman and child. But the widow mended them carefully, as if they were treasured garments, nearly new, torn by some quirk accident rather than the steady grinding of hard work. "Someday," she said to her daughter. "Someday I will be a celebrated seamstress, and you will help me cut cloth from heavy bolts of linen and wool and bright folds of silk from faraway lands. We will lay them out in a sunny room with a long table, and the breeze from the sea will dance through our window and muss the fabric if we forget to weight it with stones."

She folded the finished work and laid it in the hands of her daughter, who moved through the streets carrying the tidy bundles to their owners and returning with payment in coin or food and more shabby clothes for mending. When the daughter turned four, she began practicing coarse crooked stitches on scraps of old cloth. When she turned five, she began to help with some of the hidden stitching. The mother watched her laboring, quivering at times with frustration or exhaustion, or jerking away from the stab of a needle, and her heart ached.

When her daughter turned seven, the mother said, "If I am going to be a seamstress, you must go to school." From beneath a stone in the floor, she took a small leather sack of coins.

"No," protested the daughter. "That is our money for cloth. Our first bolt. You promised."

"I was wrong," said the mother. "If I am to be a seamstress, I will need an assistant who can measure, who can read numbers and words and can write. An assistant who can keep track of what is paid and what is due. A bolt of cloth can come after. First things first."

That night the mother warmed a basin of water and scrubbed her daughter from head to toe. She trimmed her nails and rebraided her hair. She washed the girl's dress carefully so as not to fray it more and hung it over the chair to dry.

In the morning, they walked to the house of a teacher who had a second-story room that served as a school. Most of his students were boys and most came from more prosperous households, but the teacher admired the widow's determination so he agreed to teach the girl. He showed them the classroom. The mother nodded quietly at the worn pine floor and long benches and wide window with sunlight streaming through, and she traded the coins for a slate and a year's tuition.

Gradually, the girl learned to read and write. Ever conscious of the cost, she labored over the letters as her mother labored over the mending. Head bent, she traced the curves over until they looked to her like art, graceful white patterns on the black of her slate. Then, as the letters began clustering themselves into familiar words, she discovered something delightful that no one had told her: *Written words have colors!* Alone, the letters remained white on black or, when she stitched them into a sampler to hang above the bed, black on white. But her name, in the same black thread on the same white muslin, was, as always, a wonderful shade of rose.

"Look," she said to her mother. "Isn't my name beautiful?"

"It *is* beautiful," said the mother, and she traced the shapes with her fingers.

"No," said the daughter, "I mean the color."

The mother looked confused. "Did you use a different thread for your name?" she asked.

"No," said the girl, disappointed. "I guess you can't see the color because you don't know how to read."

One day, she tried to ask her teacher about it. "How much will my mother need to learn before she too can see the colors in words?"

At first he looked puzzled. Then he laughed and commented on the imaginings of children. Then, when she persisted, he became stern and said, "Such nonsense is for those who wander the streets talking to themselves and to the birds. Unless you can live on imaginary bread in an imaginary house, you'd best stick to the meanings of words rather than their colors."

She also asked a classmate after school one day about the color of words. He too reacted oddly, like he didn't understand. When she finally made her question clear, he backed away and shook his head at her, and then he turned and hurried after a cluster of boys who had left the school ahead of them. Finally, it dawned on her: *Others do not see the colors!* After that, she didn't talk about the colors of words, though they continued to delight her.

As the girl's reading became more fluent so that the meanings of written words leapt unbidden into her consciousness, colors leapt out along with the meanings, and her gray surroundings became festive and bright. She loved the flow that emanated from her teacher's chalk on the blackboard. She loved the rainbow of street signs that she passed as she carried mending from her home to the surrounding neighborhoods. Best of all, she loved the hues of the ships' names she saw painted on the docked vessels.

In the evenings, as she sat stitching with her mother by candlelight or copying equations over on her slate, her talk was all about color, though not the colors of words. She talked about pink pansies pushing out through a crack in a stucco wall, of purple plumes on a hat she had seen through a carriage window, of brown and orange spices ground at the market. But now she carefully kept to herself what were the most beautiful things of all: a family name stenciled onto the wall next to the pansies, the lettering on the carriage, the labels attached to the bags of spices.

Near the girl's home was a public square where several narrow streets converged around a fountain. The half-circular basin rested against a stone retaining wall that was built when the port city began to curl its way up a steep cliff. Low in the wall, water poured from a conch shell which supported a magnificent mermaid. The mermaid held a sword in one hand and a shield in the other, to symbolize the power and protectiveness of the Sea Goddess. And above the mermaid's head, twice the fountain's width and higher even than that, words covered the wall, stained by lichens and grime, chipped and cracked through in places, but mostly legible. Farther out, fragments of protruding stone suggested that a ceiling and walls had once sheltered the fountain, but these were long vanished.

One day, it occurred to the girl to visit the square. She knew the place, had known it since she was small, had passed by it many times with her mother on their way to the market or to visit a distant relative during a ritual of birthing or sending. But she had not seen the fountain or its engraved words since she became a reader.

She hurried through her deliveries, planning her route so that she could stop by the fountain on her way home. At last, she set her bundle on a wide stone block where the basin met the wall, and backed away, staring upward at the majestic mermaid.

The words appeared gray to her at first, as she struggled to make them out. But as she persisted, she began to recognize first a few and then many words, and they started to come alive:

In Death as in Birth,
Bathed in the [   ] of Life,
We Have [   ] Our Sons to the Sea of Our Fathers,
Our [   ] to the Dark of Night …

So began a long poem. She recognized it as tribute to those fallen in an ancient ocean battle and to the city itself. But the message was confusing. There were words she didn't know, names she couldn't pronounce, and unfamiliar events.

Finally she realized that the sky was darkening, and she must be on her way. She drank from the fountain and gathered up her bundle. As she was leaving, she glanced back up at the wall, which now had a scattering of color. She laughed. "I will learn *all* these words," she said to the mermaid, "and this will be the most beautiful wall in the city. More beautiful than the mansions of the lords. More beautiful than the royal palace. More beautiful than the Temple of Knowledge. And only you and I will know." Straining in the fading light, she memorized the letters of an unfamiliar word and started back through the streets toward home.

"What is it you are deciphering?" asked her teacher after the third or fourth time that she quizzed him on the meaning of some memorized fragment of the script.

"An inscription," she answered, with an edge of secretive pride in her voice.

"Well, bring as many questions as you like," he said, pleased by her curiosity. And she did, all through the next year when he kept her in school out of kindness (and in exchange for having his laundry tended and his floors swept clean). And she asked questions through the following year, when she helped him with bookkeeping (which he took in on the side). And through the next year, when she tutored the youngest students separately during the first part of the day.

By then she had long since finished her translation of the poem. Many of the words were names of places and of heroes. The teacher had kindly woven their stories into his history lessons so that when she visited the square and gazed upon them, all the words became meaningful, each with its vivid hue. *Did he know the gift he had given her?*, she wondered.

On the day after she deciphered the last unfamiliar phrase, she stood before the fountain. Now the wall was more beautiful than she had dreamed it. "If you could only turn your head," she said to the mermaid, "You would see that you are surrounded by all the colors of creation." She read the poem aloud to the mermaid, and though several passersby stopped to listen, she read on till she was finished.

After that, she came to the fountain as often as she could. It was her place, the place where she could share her secret with the mermaid. The words sang through her mind, and the colors danced in patterns till they formed new poetry of their own, some only in greens and blues, some in rich warm colors, some in a metallic monochrome. She imagined that the rain washed the colors down the wall and into the fountain where she drank them in and carried them home to brighten the long late evenings of dim-lit stitching.

At the end of five years, the girl had completed her schooling. She stood with three adolescent boys in a room of younger students and parents, including her own mother in a borrowed dress. One by one, the teacher presented certificates, complimenting each recipient on the skills and strengths he would carry into the world or, for those most privileged, into the next phase of studies.

"And now," he said turning with a smile to the small audience, "our last graduate is a young lady with a great love of words and of history and an even greater imagination. She will recite *The Tribute of Andarius I*, an epic poem about the warriors and citizens who withstood the Great Siege."

The next day she was offered a position in a print shop. (It would be years before she wondered what the offer had cost her teacher in favors asked and promised.)

"You must take it," said her mother.

"No!" said the girl. "Now I can work with you during the day and get paid for it. We can save back the coins and get that bolt of cloth. We can move to a bigger room with a seaside window and buy that long table. Our business will grow faster, much faster when people see the work we can do together."

"If you can save money sewing, you can save money printing," said the mother. "We will get the bolt of cloth soon enough." She turned her back, rubbing her hand across her blurry eyes and the ache in her temples, hoping her daughter missed the gesture.

So the girl went to work in the print shop, surrounded by color and by words etched in carefully sculpted phrases. She kept ledgers and she proofed text using a dictionary that held more of her language than she had ever thought possible. At night she stitched, and she told her mother stories of the customers and the work and the curiosities that passed through her hands on fresh-inked parchment.

When the girl was fifteen, a war started. The conflict crept closer to the city walls until, as in the days of old, the city lay under siege. The work at the print shop dwindled and the wages with it. The girl and her mother could no longer add coins to their bag, and the daughter worried that her mother seemed more and more weary.

One day the girl stopped by the fountain. She gazed up at the wall, mouthing words so that the colors jumped out strong and clear. She bent to drink, drawing in the cold water, imagining as she had for so long that the colors filled her, flooding through her, drowning the discouragement and fear in which she herself of late had been drowning.

Straightening, she noticed a man standing beside her in a soldier's garb. He was not an old man, nor young. Creases at the corners of his eyes suggested he had spent years in the ocean sun, reading the horizon. Now he squinted at the inscription, straining to make out the words beneath their camouflage of time. "In death as in birth, bathed in the fluids of life …" He hesitated.

"We have offered our sons to the sea of our fathers," the girl responded. She stopped, embarrassed.

"No," said the soldier. "Please go on." So she did, faltering at first, then bold, forgetting herself in the pleasure of the familiar cadences and sounds.

"Thank you," said the man vaguely when her voice had faded. He seemed far away. His eyes retraced the chiseled script. "Lord Andarius," he groaned, as if to himself, "if ever we have needed to know your secret, it is now. Did you leave us no sign?"

"What secret?" asked the girl, suddenly alert. Somewhat unexpectedly, the man turned to her and answered.

"Do you remember how the Great Siege was broken, and with it the war?"

"Yes," said the girl. "They slipped out of the city. Andarius and a band of men. From here they made their way to a slope across the valley where they hid, emerging in the darkness before dawn. They took the enemy by stealth, killing officers, putting on the uniforms of the slain men, and calling contradictory and impossible orders. And as the sun rose, soldiers flooded from the city gates, decimating the legions who were fighting each other in panicked disarray."

"They *tunneled* out of the city," corrected the man, "though it was not widely known at the time and few history books record it. The tunnel was built at great cost in lives over a period of years. It was held in grave secrecy, and Andarius meant that it should be kept that way. All involved swore oaths that its location would die with them, and Andarius himself vowed that he would pass the secret only to his successor. But the books tell us that he died at sea, his son, Andarius II, a babe in arms.

"These past months, as our stores grow thin, a search has been made of the records in the Great Library and in the royal palace, but no document has been found that might reveal the place of the tunnel. *Look* at this tribute." He made a gesture of simultaneous respect and frustration. "He was a man of words, as fluent a poet as ever has risen among our people. If only he had left us a message."

The girl began shaking. She looked back at wall. Yes, it was still there, in bold shades of yellow. "He did," she said quietly. "It is here, I didn't know what it meant." Aloud, she read, "Beneath-flow-beside-pool-behind-center-stone-downward-outward-sunlight-unknown."

To each side of the fountain, against the wall, three massive stones lay end to end, carved on the front with a frieze. To the left, the top of the blocks held a channel hollowed into the surface of the stone. This carried the overflow from the pool until it spilled into a gutter that ran down the side of one of the approaching streets.

The soldier looked at the stones as if he had never seen them before. Then he looked back at the poem, where the words lay, mottled gray among many others. "Hidden within the old temple," he murmured. "Of course!" Then he turned and asked the girl, "How did you know?" He demanded, "How *do* you know?"

She opened her mouth to explain, but the responses to her innocent childhood questions rolled over her, flooding her with confusion and shame. "I can't tell you," she stammered, backing away. "Maybe I am wrong. I – I have to go."

"Wait," said the man, gentle now. "Maybe also you are right. Here." He fumbled, tugging a ring from his finger. Catching her arm, he pressed it into her hand. "Take this next week to the captain of the king's guard. Tell him Bern gave it to you. If you are wrong, he will thank you kindly for it. If you are right, then you are the messenger of our fathers . . . and of our fate."

That night, a rough wooden shelter was erected over and around the fountain, ringed by a guard of young soldiers. The local people stretched and craned, but couldn't see through to the activity they could hear within the walls. "This place was sacred to Andarius I, who broke the Great Siege," confided one of the guards to an inquisitive girl with a pretty smile. "One of the generals had a vision. Andarius promised him that if we erect a temple here, he will come to our aid and the enemy will be defeated."

The rumor spread from shop to shop and house to house.

"Our leaders are truly desperate to be putting energy into sheltering that old mermaid," muttered some. "They should be in the field, fighting. This is weakness and folly."

But others disagreed. "If we do not have the spirits of our forefathers and the powers of the Sea Goddess on our side, all else is futile."

Days passed and the work continued. Blocks of stone arrived on carts, salvaged from a shelter that was being disassembled in the royal gardens and reconstructed in the open space around the fountain. "They cannot leave the city to quarry stone," commented a woman to her husband. "Will Andarius be angry that they respond to his apparition with a garden shelter? Or will he be pleased by their haste?"

"We will know soon enough," responded the husband. "Soon enough. At least they are making a solid foundation – Andarius would be pleased with that." He pointed to a cart laden with dirt that was creaking away from the site. Then he tilted his head toward the half-built temple in a sign of deference and placed a copper coin on the tip of the mermaid's tail before continuing on his way.

In four weeks, the monument was finished. And in five, the siege. The small temple sat glistening, sunlight pouring through the open front and two side windows onto the mermaid and the mounds of offerings: coppers, flowering branches, grain, and fruit. As in the time of Andarius, the seaside army had surprised and routed the enemy by mysteriously appearing from the hillsides across the valley. The people celebrated their victory and paid homage to the unseen powers that had won their freedom.

In the sixth week, the girl presented herself at the gate to the royal palace and asked for the captain of the king's guard. "Bern told me to come here," she said, and she showed the gatekeeper the ring. He looked at it closely and then beckoned a soldier, who led her across a cobbled courtyard to a room where a man sat writing at a desk. He looked up at the sound of their approach and then stood to greet her.

The captain was neither old nor young, and when he smiled, the creases by his eyes suggested years in the ocean sun, reading the horizon. Almost instantly, she recognized him as the soldier she had met at the fountain! "I startled you," he commented. "I thought you might not come," he added.

"I am sorry," said the girl. "My mother took ill during the siege and we could find no medicine. I did not want to leave her; I could not. I very nearly lost her." Then she paused and inquired, "Why did you not say that it was you I should ask for?"

"Because I did not know if I would be among the living or with the Sea Goddess. But I knew that whoever might serve as the king's captain would know my name and the story of our encounter, and that he would treat you well.

"The tunnel was where you said it would be, as I'm sure you have guessed. It had collapsed in places, and more stone fell as we cleared the rubble. But it served us as it served Andarius." He laughed. "It is remarkable how few have felt compelled to ask how we slipped out of the city, to strike from behind. How does it feel to have changed the course of history?"

The girl flushed. "Most say it was the spirit of Andarius who cloaked you in darkness because you built the temple for the Goddess as he requested."

"And they are not altogether wrong, are they? May I ask now how you knew?"

She met him with silence. *Why was it so hard to say?*

"May I guess?" asked the captain, and she nodded. "When you read, words have colors. The words of the message were a different color than those around them, perhaps different than any other words on the wall."

The girl looked at him, wide-eyed.

He turned to his desk and picked up a single sheet of parchment. Scanning down the page, he read, "Beyond all these wishes, my son, is my heart's hope that the written word will unveil itself to you, as it has to me, in a blaze of color, in a myriad of hues and tints: the pale delicacy of the sunrise and the spring, the boldness of midsummer, the rich depth that precedes the darkness …" He paused and looked up at the girl. "It is a rare gift, almost unknown. Most scholars have thought these words were a poet's metaphor for the pleasures he found in the writings of others and in his own self expression, but I think not. Am I right?"

The girl nodded, speechless. *A gift!* A weight lifted from her that she had not known she carried. Shame, perhaps, or loneliness, or the dread of being discovered.

"Is that why you wanted to see me?" she asked, finally.

"No, I did not guess till later. There were many reasons why I might need to speak with you again – I do not even know your name." She told him. He repeated it and nodded, then paced to the window and back. He continued, "These coming weeks there will be more parades and banquets, honors of all kinds for those who died in battle and for those whose success gave meaning to their death. I wish that you might be at the front of the parades and in the banquet halls with me. However, we have gone to great lengths to leave the tunnel of Andarius as we found it – hidden. Your presence would raise unanswerable questions."

"Oh!" said the girl, nonplused. "The gift, as you have called it, was not of my own choosing. And I did not go to the fountain to help with the siege, only to soothe my own curiosity. I am not expecting honors, nor do I deserve them."

"Choosing is important," responded the man, "as is intent. But, quite frankly, so are outcomes. You have saved our city untold misery, possibly defeat. I and those around me would like to recognize your significance in some way. Is there anything I can offer you, anything you need?"

"No," said the girl, and then, "Yes." She blinked back sudden tears. "My mother used all she had saved to send me to school. She dreamed of a room by the sea with a window, and a table, and bolts of cloth that would match the quality of her stitching. Now she seems as worn as the mending she takes in from the neighbors. Maybe it is too late. Or maybe I ask too much."

"It is done," said the man. "And for yourself?"

"Come away from that window," she chided her mother, laughing. "You have been there the better part of an hour. You have the rest of your life to look out at the sea. Come over to this window. Through it, you can see the very rooms where I will be working." The mother crossed to where her daughter leaned against a freshly painted sill, pointing at the facade of the Ancient Archive, across the square from the mermaid.

"It is wonderful," she said. "But I still don't understand. You have given up nothing you will regret? You have sold nothing you will wish to reclaim? You have made no promises you cannot keep?"

"I dare not explain," said the girl. "But I told you. I have done nothing wrong, nothing to be ashamed of, and I am bound to no one. Trust me!" She gazed out the window for a while and then sighed. "I can tell you this much: I helped with the temple, with the tribute to Andarius and the Sea Goddess, but in ways I cannot describe to you. They are not my secrets to tell."

"Ah," said the mother, content at last. "I wondered if you had the vision. Since you were small you have been seeing things that others could not." She reached up to the sampler that hung on the wall beside them and brushed her fingers across her daughter's name. "Sometimes when I am stitching, I imagine what it must be like to see the world through your eyes …" She kissed her daughter on the forehead and smiled. "Now though, it is a joy to see it through my own." With that, she turned to her new work table, smoothing the fabric that had been mussed by the breeze, and began tracing a pattern onto a silk that seemed to interweave all the colors of creation.

The Quilt

Once there was a lonely girl who lived in a small town in the mountains. Her parents had died in a house fire that left her arms and face badly scarred. Her skin was red, rough and uneven, and the people of the town considered her ugly. Although elderly neighbors had taken her in, they could give the poor child little, for they had scarcely enough for themselves. They provided her with clothes that were passed on by other families, but because the old woman's eyes were too dim for sewing and the girl was too little to stitch for herself, the dresses hung crooked and lumpy on her small, scarred body.

The other children shunned her. At times they were deliberately cruel, taunting her about her skin or her clothes. But mostly they stayed away. So the girl spent most of her time alone, in body and spirit.

To help the old woman and man, the girl sometimes helped to clean the bakery in exchange for a few rolls. Sometimes she ran errands for the shop owners in return for some flour or sugar, a handful of beans or peas, or a cup of oil. When these tasks were done, many empty hours remained.

As she grew older, the loneliness and shame she felt while lingering in the town square or watching the other children play became unbearable. Yet she would not return home, because she did not want to grieve the elderly couple with her pain. Instead, she began to wander the meadows and forests above the town, seeking comfort from the mountain and her own imagination.

On the southern side of the mountain, she found the earth as scarred as she was. A river crosscut a path along that side of the mountain, where men had been cutting trees and sending them downstream to the coastal plain. The over-harvested slopes were rutted and muddy, while other slopes were dotted with tunnels and slag, evidence that miners had been searching for gold on the exposed mountainside.

To the north, though, the forests lay untouched. There, alone with the aspen trees and lupines and watercress and blueberries and all the small inhabitants of the mountain, the girl could feel at peace. One day, she followed a deer path she had never explored before, and she found a crystal-clear pool. A stream cascaded off the hillside above, and behind the falling water the rocky wall seemed to disappear. The girl swam in the pool and then pushed through the curtain of water to find a small dry cave on the other side.

This, declared the girl to herself, *is my special place, my heart's home!* She thanked the Mountain Spirit for allowing her to discover it and asked for his permission to make it her sanctuary. She was certain he both heard and answered her prayer.

After that, the girl came to the cave often, whenever her tasks and the weather allowed. In the fall, though, it became too cold to swim, and the girl worried that she would not be able to get into her cave again until spring. She was resourceful, however, and one day she climbed above the waterfall to inspect how the water flowed over the rocks. She discovered that by wedging a sapling between the boulders, she could divert the water's flow to one side, such that she could enter the cave without soaking herself in the cascade. Thus, she had a door made of water that she could open when she arrived and close when she returned home. Her sanctuary was now available to her in all seasons.

At first the wild animals that used the pool were frightened by her presence and fled, but she saved for them what she could from her earnings – a few crumbs or an occasional pocketful of grain. Because they were attentive in ways that humans are not, the animals sensed the goodness in her. Within a few months or less, the animals came freely to her. Even the deer would lick salty crumbs or sweet berry juice from her fingers, and eventually they let her stroke their sleek necks. Sometimes an animal came to her injured. Then she would tend it carefully, cleaning and binding wounds with strips of her own tattered garments if need be.

Though she was cradled in the majesty of the mountain, the girl could never quite forget her own scars. One day, when she caught her reflection in the pool, she said to herself: *Oh, if only I could be one of the deer, sleek and smooth. If only I could be one of the aspens, soft and shimmering. If only I could be the water of the pool, reflecting the sky and the earth and the spirits around me.* Tears fell down her face into the pool, distorting the reflections and blending together shapes and colors.

Suddenly, an idea came to her. "I will make a quilt," she said aloud, "a quilt of the life in this forest, and I will cloak myself in it, so that I too may be beautiful!" Once again, she was certain that the Mountain Spirit heard her call.

She began her project by carving a needle from a splinter of old bone. Then, she wove a cord from the grasses that grew at the edge of the pond and started stitching together little bits and pieces of the forest itself. It was late summer, so she stitched fronds of yarrow, blue lupines, and creamy bark from the aspen trees. Her damaged fingers were twisted and awkward, so the process was slow. But crafting the quilt made her happy, and she sang merrily as she stitched. When the light grew dusky, she carefully tucked away her work inside the cave, and hurried back to town.

For several days, she could not return to the forest, for there was work to be had in one of the shops. When she did return, she was surprised to find the colors in the quilt as bright as ever, the flowers unfaded and the leaves unwilted. And so it would be, all through the long days of summer. During each visit, she would take out her quilt and find it as fresh as if she had stitched it only that morning, and each day she would add a little bit more.

In the fall she added golden aspen leaves, green stems of cress, bright red leaves from the berry bushes, and a blue jay feather. *Surely*, she thought, *I will finish before winter. Then I will wrap myself in my quilt, and I will dance!* But the chill winds came early, and the girl had to leave, knowing she would not return till the snows melted. She laid her quilt tenderly in the cave, and, climbing the hill to move the sapling, closed the door of water for the winter.

That winter was long. The winds blew harshly from the south, and the town was plagued by illness. Much to the girl's sorrow, first the elderly man and then the elderly woman joined their ancestors during those cold dark months. Now she was truly alone. After the rites of passage, she spent her days in solitude, listlessly tending the fire or preparing her meals, waiting for spring.

As the cruel weather wore on, the people began to grumble. Something is wrong, they said. Never have we had a winter so harsh. Someone must have offended the gods. The council members, mostly merchants and foresters and guildsmen, were called together, but they could see no reason for nature's anger. A priest was consulted, but he merely eyed the gathered company, collected their gold, then muttered a prophecy that was indecipherable.

"I know what's wrong," said the girl, when she overheard two of the townspeople speculating in worried tones at the well. But they merely stared at her and then resumed their conversation as if she hadn't spoken.

Finally, the cold broke, and a warm thawing breeze blew in from the coast. But it offered no relief, for as the snow began to melt, dark churning currents of muddy water came rushing down the mountainside, flooding much of the small valley that held the town, and sweeping away the houses and shops closest to the river.

The townspeople gathered in the square, weary from the battle with the elements, frightened and angry. "What is to be done?" they asked, and "Who is to blame?"

"I know what's wrong," repeated the girl, and this time the crowd turned to listen. "The mountain is wounded above the town," she said. "It is bleeding. We have scarred it and made it ugly. The Mountain Spirit is offended."

The people stared at her. Then someone shouted, "It is your own ugliness that offends the gods."

"Yes," muttered others, some because they did not want to hear her reproof, and some because they did not want to hear it from her, the lowest among them, and some because they could not see beyond her skin and thought the accusation fitting.

A dark mutter rose, and people moved away from the girl. Then a boy, jeering, threw a stone. The girl backed away, terrified, and as she turned to flee, the people grabbed stones all around her and struck her and drove her from the town, badly hurt.

She made her way to the pool and, unable to climb the hill above, rushed through the curtain of water. She collapsed, soaked, but it seemed warm to her inside the cave, and the aching in her body faded along with the last of her strength. She reached for the quilt and drew it over herself. As she did, she noticed dimly that somehow it had been completed for her, with tender shoots of snow lily and crocus and fiddle heads of fern, the plants of the early spring. Nestled in her cave and covered in her quilt, she released her soul to sleep.

Outside, the wind screamed. The water poured down the mountainside in torrents that drove many townspeople to abandon their homes permanently, lest they ever experience another calamity like this one. But the girl knew none of this.

When she awoke, the sun shone in through the cave opening and the curtain of water had been drawn aside. A young man sat beside her, unknown to her and yet somehow familiar. "I have been waiting for you," he said.

"Who are you?" asked the girl, unafraid.

"I am the Mountain Spirit," he answered. "I have taken your form so that you can take mine. Come." He reached out his hand, and she sat up, surprised that she could move with ease. Then, abruptly, she drew back and clutched the quilt tightly around her, hanging her head so that her hair fell over her face.

"Why are you hiding?" he asked.

"Because I am ugly," she said, ashamed.

"No, you are not. Look." He helped her up, and leading her to the cave entrance pointed to her reflection in the pool. She looked and saw that she had been made whole. Not only the wounds from the stones were gone, but also her old scars.

She put her hand to her cheek. "You have made me beautiful," she said with wonder.

"No," he replied. "You always were." Then he kissed her forehead, and she was transformed into the spirit form of the gods. The two rose above the pool, above the mountain, and danced on the wind.

Afterward, he took the quilt from her shoulders and cast it from the sky. As it fell, the quilt grew larger and larger. The girl watched it grow in size and then land, a soft patchwork of color covering the treeless slopes, the scars in the mountainside, the overflowing river. At once, the magical quilt infused the landscape and calmed the river.

And life began anew.

The Shepherd

A shepherd from the highlands went to the coast to buy a new breed of sheep, recently arrived from the western isles. On an afternoon with an ominous sky and rising wind, he found what he was looking for in the great market at the port. He bought a ewe with a lamb still suckling, two more ewes, and a ram. He tied the sheep on leads and set off for his guesthouse where he would keep them in the courtyard till his other tasks in the city were finished.

The animals were uneasy because of the weather. When thunder cracked offshore, the ram butted the shepherd into the edge of a rusted iron gate. A jagged edge of metal sliced through his trousers and into his calf. In the two days that followed, as he completed other purchases and prepared for the return home, his leg ached and swelled, and streaks of red ran up and down from the cut, so that finally, at the insistence of his host, the shepherd consulted a doctor before beginning his journey home.

"Drink this infusion twice daily," said the doctor. "And water in between, whether you feel thirsty or not. In the evening, apply the poultices as hot as you can stand them. The rest of the day, keep your leg bound with the ointment covering the wound."

The doctor seemed tired, anxious to be finished with this patient who had come late in the day. As he spoke, a cloth bundle that lay on a table beside them made a small sound and stirred. Part of the cloth fell aside and two dark eyes stared up at the shepherd.

"A baby," he said, surprised.

"Two of them," said the doctor. "Their mother was brought in from a ship that wrecked in the storm two nights ago. She died today, giving birth. The monks from the crematorium took her body, but they wouldn't take the babies live. It falls on me to expose them." He looked grim.

"You can't find anyone who will take them?" asked the shepherd. He looked away from the dark eyes and then back again.

"No," said the doctor. Bitterness edged into his voice. "I have spent the day trying. They are female. They are foreign. They are early. Even if I found a wet nurse, they might not survive. But there is no nurse. People in these parts think that the death of a mother is an omen and that the child who brings evil in birth will bring evil in life. If the infant is a relative, they may persuade themselves otherwise, find other ways to justify the misfortune. No such luck for these two … Are you finished? I would like to be done with my work."

The shepherd stared down at the bundle. "Can they live on sheep's milk?" he asked.

"Probably not," said the doctor.

The two men stood in silence, neither moving. "Well," said the shepherd, "I will take them anyway. They can as easily die with the sheep as with the wolves." He shoved into his pocket the packets of herbs and ointment that he had been holding, and picked up the bundle off of the table, unwrapping enough to reveal another little head with eyes closed. He nodded awkwardly at the doctor and moved toward the door.

"Wait," said the doctor. He held out the coins that the shepherd had paid him for treatment, then, reaching into a jar on the counter, handed him a few more.

The matron of the guesthouse clicked her tongue when she realized what the shepherd had brought home. "It is better for them to die at once than to waste away slowly," she said. "You've only brought yourself pain. Look at those little bodies, barely bigger than your hand." Nevertheless, the matron cleaned the infants and wrapped them in fresh cloth. Then she sent her daughter down the street to a neighbor who was almost ready to wean her third child.

"I'll do it," said the neighbor. "It's a good excuse for the weaning. But not for long."

The shepherd laid the babies on the floor beside his bed that night, two white bundles on top of his coat. He lay awake, listening to a small rasping cry. "At least you won't die alone and cold," he said. "At least you had a full stomach once."

But they didn't die. A month later, the shepherd arrived at his village, provisions bound onto his back and a linen sheet tied into a pouch on his front. Before him trotted his small flock of sheep, including a ewe who was nursing three instead of one.

"You of all people!" said his sister. "How many times have you killed a lamb born wrong? Nature herself does the same."

"They wanted to live," said the shepherd. And that was all the explanation he ever offered, for in truth, he had none. How could he explain what had passed between himself and the twins – with those round soulful eyes – on the first day of their lives?

The sister was a good woman, generous and kind, but with a muted edge of grief. Married fifteen years, she and her husband were childless. After her brother appeared with his foundlings, she often found herself raw with the pain of her barren years. But as time went on, the dark brown-eyed baby and her green-eyed sister crept into her heart, and she realized they had not only reopened her wound but had also healed it.

The village made space for the shepherd's newly acquired family. A friend took his sheep to the high summer pastures with his own flock so that the shepherd could stay in town, working the fields of a neighboring farmer in exchange for winter fodder. The sister and her husband added a sleeping loft on the top of their house. "You must winter with us," they said. "You can't leave the babies alone when you care for your animals, and you can't take them with you into the blowing snow."

So it was that the two girls became children of the village. When their adoptive father could no longer carry them both on his back while he worked, they toddled after their aunt or played at her feet, stacking pebbles and pine cones while she wove at her loom. As they grew, they chased falling leaves in the streets in the fall and diverted streamlets in the sheep pasture in the spring. They struggled with chubby fingers to get a needle through cloth or to shell peas for cooking.

In their sixth year, after a fierce battle between their father and aunt over whether they were ready, the twins also became children of the summer pastures. They roamed with the flock and slept in stone huts that were shared by other shepherds. Under their father's tutelage, they began to learn the plants of the high meadows, edibles and healing herbs, and they began to wrestle with the crossbow. "You think you can start with two female orphans and end up with two sons," sneered a gray-haired goatherd from another valley. "Perhaps," said the father.

That fall, he enrolled the twins in the village school. It was there that they first learned the circumstances of their birth. The aunt knew as soon as they walked through the door that something was wrong. "What is it?" she asked, setting down her shuttle. She stood and crossed the room to where the two girls stood, eyes averted. "What is it?" she demanded again. She caught the green-eyed sister by the chin and lifted the small face to meet her gaze.

"The children say we are cursed," said the girl, beginning to cry. "They say we killed our mother . . . and that we are going to kill Father too. We should have been left to die."

"Oh," said the aunt, with a choking sound as if she had been hit. She wrapped her arm around the child and caught the sister with her other arm. They tolerated her attempts at soothing them, her fierce denials and her reassurances, but they were not convinced. When their father came home, he tried to reassure them too. He told the girls what he knew about their birth, wishing that he had told them sooner. He struggled to find the right words so that they would be protected against the accusations of their peers.

"It was a terrible storm, as bad as any I've known. The ship was driven onto rocks off the coast. They say a lighthouse signaled for help, but no one could get out of the harbor. I don't know how your mother made it ashore. I can only think that her will to bring you into this world gave her the strength to keep swimming. Without you inside of her, she might have died that much sooner. But instead of dying for nothing, she died giving you life, the most precious of gifts. What you can give in return is to live your lives well." The girls nodded, but the shepherd worried that they did so only out of respect.

In the days that followed, the twins moped, unreachable. First one, then the other stopped eating the mutton that was a substantial part of the highland diet. "Beat them," said a neighbor, in response to the shepherd's frustrations. "They'll start eating fast enough."

"No," said the shepherd. "After I left the city, they were suckled by a sheep that was later slaughtered. They must fear that they live by the death of all who nurture them." He didn't beat the girls, but he did keep trying to persuade them. "Living takes life," he repeated at dinner. "All animals compete, and we draw our nourishment from other living beings. It is the way of the world." The girls listened politely, respectfully, but continued their fast of meat.

Finally, the shepherd took them to the healer in a neighboring village. She was a dark, shriveled woman who drew on the powers of herbs and potions and (some said) incantations that invoked the spirits of the earth itself. "Cure them," he pleaded. "Make them understand. Tell them they were born for a purpose."

The old woman scrutinized the two girls with eyes that reminded the shepherd oddly of the newborn who had compelled his gaze years before. Side by side, clutching each other's hands, the twins stared back at her. After a long time, the healer spoke. "They were not born for *a* purpose," she said. "But if they seek, *many* purposes, great and small, will present themselves and ask to be chosen." Then she fell silent again.

"Yes, yes," said the shepherd, annoyed with her riddles and long silences. He was disappointed that the half-day's journey had not produced the ally he so desperately needed. "Can you at least tell them to eat? They are not going to find any of those purposes unless they are strong and healthy."

"They look healthy and strong to me," said the healer. "There are many sources of nourishment. They will eat flesh if they need to, when the time comes. You have two powerful daughters. When they decide where they are going, they will know what they need to do."

"Have you nothing more to offer us?" asked the shepherd.

"Yes," said the old woman. "This tea was given to me by someone special. It is made of spices that were brought across the sea. I think the three of you will find it delightful as you relax together by your evening hearth."

Very little was said on the long walk home. "That was time and money wasted," the shepherd confided in frustration to his sister. Even so, as they sat sipping the last of the tea a week later, it occurred to him that the distance between the girls and the family had dissolved away somehow. Though the sisters continued in their odd diet, he found that he didn't mind.

So the girls ate as they chose, and, in spite of the worries of their elders, continued growing and learning. During the summers in the high meadows, both became proficient with the crossbow so that they could protect the sheep if need be. But they refused to hunt the ptarmigan and rabbits and occasional deer with which the shepherd supplemented their meals of porridge and summer berries.

One summer night, the girls sat by the fire with their father and a neighboring shepherd who shared their camp. The late setting sun had left the sky dark gray rather than blue, and the moon could cast no shadows on an eerie landscape of silhouettes. Suddenly, a lamb cried out. A black shape carrying a small white bundle leapt over the stone wall that enclosed the sheep, and the lamb cried out again in terror and pain. The father cursed and jumped to his feet. Snatching up his crossbow, he ran after the disappearing shape. Both daughters bolted after him, leaving their flock in the care of the neighbor.

Across the broad meadow the wolf ran, past blackened forms of lone trees and rocks, following a game trail that led into the steep treed hillside where he might lose his pursuers and kill and devour his prey. The shepherd shouted as he ran, hoping that in his haste to escape, the wolf would drop the lamb. He too, was familiar with the game trail, and when the wolf vanished into the trees, he did the same, still following the calls of the lamb. Beneath the trees, the girls could see nothing, and they blindly followed the sounds of their father ahead.

Suddenly there was the rumble of a rock slide ahead of them; then all became still. "Father! Father!" they called, panicked. But there was no response. They fumbled for the path and then pushed forward in the direction from which they had heard the noise. The underbrush became thicker and they knew they were off the trail.

"Where is he?" whimpered the green-eyed girl.

"Keep following the curve of the mountainside," panted her brown-eyed sister.

They fought through the underbrush, branches raking their arms and faces. Just when the trees seemed impossibly tangled, the twins burst out onto an open slope of loose boulders and scree. There, a few meters beyond and below them, lay the lamb, mewling quietly. They scrambled down to it, and the brown-eyed sister bent and ran her hand over its sticky, heaving side. Then she picked it up. The wolf was gone.

The green-eyed sister peered into the shadows. "Father!" she called again. But there was no answer. "Father!" she screamed again, this time even louder. The next moment, they heard a moan.

They followed the sound and found their father with his head bleeding and one leg pinned under a boulder. "I am fine," he said, but they could tell by his voice that he was not. "Can you can get the rock off?" he asked. While they struggled unsuccessfully to move the giant rock, he lay with one hand on the lamb and the other clenched in a fist against the pain.

"I will go for help," said the green-eyed sister at last, and she ran back through the trees and across the big meadow, stumbling through the darkness that was now complete. Finally, she reached the neighbor who was tending the sheep. He listened as she sobbed her story, then he gathered up water and blankets and said, "We will wrap your father in the blankets because we should not move him in the dark." But inside the neighbor was thinking, *in case I can't move the stone.*

When they reached the shepherd he was barely conscious, and the brown-eyed sister was trembling. The neighbor tried to move the rock, but just as he feared, he could not. All that he could do was bind the shepherd's wound, cover him, and take the injured lamb back to its mother.

This time it was the brown-eyed sister who ran for help. She ran down the hillside, jogged over the meadow and past the camp, and stumbled along the stream valley through the night, reaching the village as the sun arose. She collapsed into the arms of her aunt, who quickly organized a rescue party that set out across the valley with horses and rope, led by the brown-eyed daughter. Another team set off to fetch a bone setter, and still another group ran to get the aged healer.

Through that long night of waiting and hoping, the green-eyed sister sat with her father. She held his hand and gave him water. She talked with and sang to him. Finally, as the sky started lightening and he again lost consciousness, she sat quietly with her legs folded and the crossbow in her lap, pouring into him her will to live.

Not long after, a buck emerged from the woods on the far side of the rocky slope. It crossed the scree, then stopped at the edge of the rock slide. The girl watched the deer for a while, and then slowly raised the bow. When the neighboring shepherd came back to check on them, he was astounded to see the dead deer lying on the slope above the girl and her father. "He will need meat to heal," was all she said.

The party from the village led by the brown-eyed daughter arrived before noon. They freed the shepherd's leg, twisted and swollen, and prepared a stretcher for the long descent. *He will not live*, they thought, but as the twins watched their every move, they did not speak it. One of the men cleaned the deer and bound it to one of the horses. Carefully, methodically, the team set off again for the village.

Weeks passed, long weeks of pain and infection, of nights and days blurring into each other in an eternity of discomfort. The healer stayed with the family during this time, as her skills were desperately needed. One day the old woman could sense the shepherd emerging from his long, restless sleep. His spirit had returned. She smiled so wide that her face creased and her eyes became barely visible. When at last their eyes met, she told the shepherd of his daughters' endurance, cunning, and bravery. Now he smiled as well.

"They saved my life!" said the father to the aged healer.

"You saved your own life," she clarified, "when you picked up that bundle of babies and walked out of the doctor's office twelve years ago."

"They saved my life," repeated the father with tears of joy in his eyes.

"I know," she said. "I saw that they would. If my vision runs true, you are the first of many. As I revealed to you years ago, the girls have more than one purpose."

The Guardian

Along time ago, the plains that run down to the ocean were covered with dense forests. Back then, there were fewer people in the world, and though towns and villages clustered along the shore, the inner lands belonged to the wild animals. A traveler might walk a fortnight on trails made by elk and bear before finding an inhabited valley in the foothills of the great mountains. In one such valley, though, a small village had grown up, surrounded by the vast sea of ancient trees.

The people there worked together, tending gardens of summer vegetables, hunting, raising a small flock of sheep or a few cows, and maintaining the structures of the village itself. When a roof needed mending, a man called his wife and his neighbors and children and they all assisted in the repair. The hunters went out in groups of two or three, and when they returned, villagers joined together to divide and preserve the kill. They built dams and traps for a nearby stream to harvest the fish that lived there. In this way they were able to support a smith, a tailor, a potter, and a midwife who knew the mysterious herbs of light and darkness. Finally – and this was their proudest accomplishment – they built a school which also served as a meeting hall.

But survival was a struggle. The villagers lost not only sheep but also young children to the wolves and cougars that came down from the mountains. Sometimes a garden would be ravaged by a bear who found the vegetables to be tasty and easy picking. When the winter freeze was particularly hard and deep, most of the fish died in the stream, and it took years for them to recover enough that the villagers dared to harvest again. If the snows came early or stayed too long, the people knew hunger, and fevers struck down the frail and elderly. Then, in the first deep thaws, those remaining devoted themselves, with gaunt faces and weakened arms, to burying the dead.

One summer while the hunters were out, highwaymen from the coast stumbled across the village. They had discovered that isolated hamlets were easy prey, and this one was no exception. They demanded food and clothing, which the people of the village provided. Then the robbers took whatever else they would from the humble homes, as the women and children could offer little resistance. When the hunters returned they found the highwaymen gone and the village full of sorrow and anger.

With these emotions hanging heavy over them, the elders closed themselves in the meeting hall to determine what should be done. Long they discussed the hardships they had borne for generations, including this most recent assault. "We need protection," they said, "the suffering is too great, the losses too many. And neither our weapons nor our incantations have the power to safeguard those who are young and weak among us." They had heard of a man who had knowledge beyond their own in the realm of sorcery and magic, and after much debate, they sent a messenger to find him.

Within a fortnight, the man came. He was a young man, ageless rather, with shrewd eyes and an expression that was unreadable. "I can help you," he said. "I am a sculptor. I can create for you a guardian and breathe into it the power you seek. But it will cost you." He scanned the anxious faces of the gathered company and named a price in gold. It was the sum of all they owned in jewelry and coin, both what they had inherited and what they had earned through their occasional exchanges with peddlers or travelers. Then he averted his gaze and began studying the roof and lines of the meeting hall, his posture saying clearly that the price was not open to discussion.

The villagers withdrew and consulted together in muffled tones. "He is greedy," said some. "He is a charlatan," said others. "We should give him nothing but provisions for his return home," one shouted.

But an influential elder spoke next. "We made a decision," he said. "Have you forgotten how many we buried in the early thaw? Do you remember the child who disappeared last summer, along with three lambs? Need I remind you of our helplessness when the robbers came?"

The midwife, a stooped and wrinkled woman who worked by small magic and great skill and still greater intuition, agreed. "Greedy he may be, and I cannot see his soul's quest, but he is no charlatan. If we pay him for power he will be able to draw power to us." So they said to the sculptor, "We need what we need. We will pay what you ask."

He demanded the meeting hall as a work space and a living space, and they consented. The children were busy with the tasks of summer, weeding the gardens, working alongside their parents on the irrigation channels and the fish pond, harvesting reeds for baskets and traps, binding grasses for thatch. They wouldn't need the classroom till the harvest was in and the first frost was on the ground. The people carried out the benches and slates, bringing in a cot for sleeping, a rough table and chair for meals, a basin for washing, and, finally, the first materials the sculptor requested for his work: a wooden platform about as long and wide as a man is tall, bundles of hay, and mounds of clay, strained and wedged, prepared for shaping. "The rest will come later," he said. Then he sent them away.

The next day the sculptor began work, piling the hay on top of the platform and then smoothing clay over it. He called for more, and then again for more. They brought all the clay that their village potter had stored, mixing and kneading it to just the right consistency so that it could be added to the growing mound. Even that wasn't enough, and two women were sent with baskets and pack frames to bring more. They carried it from an eroded bank several miles away where the clay was fine and smooth and good for firing.

Before the clay was taken to the man, it was prepared by the village potter and her apprentice. For two weeks they worked on sifting and mixing and kneading clay, and bringing it to the sculptor, one basket at a time. Finally, one afternoon, as the apprentice emptied yet another heavy load onto the platform beside the mound, the sculptor stepped back, looked the whole thing over with a critical eye, and said, "That's enough."

The potter's apprentice was a boy named Cub. That wasn't his real name; they called him that because one of his legs bent and turned in, giving him a funny loping gait. "Like a bear cub," they said. The malformed leg made it harder for him to walk to and from the gardens and the ponds. That is why he was apprenticed to the potter. He knew how to grind pigments and glazes. He knew how to make sure that the wet clay forms didn't dry too quickly. He knew how to form basic shapes like small bowls and plates. And he knew how to smooth off the rough edges that were left when the potter used a stylus to carve decorative patterns on the outsides of pitchers and urns.

Now the sculptor turned to him. "I need an assistant," he said. "What do you know about making forms for casting?" Cub stammered slightly. He feared the sculptor, and yet the thought of helping to create the village guardian was beyond his dreams. He listed his skills. "Good," said the man. "You will keep the clay covered and damp. You will bring me what I need. You will tell the villagers only what I instruct you to tell them about my work. And if you make me angry …" he gave Cub a long dark look. "If you make me angry I will see to it that your good leg matches the other." Cub turned pale, but he stood his ground. He nodded in agreement.

So it was that Cub joined the sculptor as his assistant. If food and water were brought by the villagers, Cub was the one who carried them from the door and arranged them on the table. If tools needed cleaning or sharpening, Cub was the one who carried them to the well and sat in the square with a whetstone, smoothing and honing the edges. Cub slept on a mat beside the platform, awakening during the night to feel the damp cloth that covered the evolving creation, making sure that the clay didn't dry out. And when a large winged lion began emerging from the lumps and mounds beneath the cloth, Cub was the one who saw it first and the only one from the village who saw it up close.

Cub grew to dislike the sculptor. The man spoke little except to give directions, and his moods were often dark. He seemed to like giving orders, and worse, he seemed to enjoy the fact that Cub feared him. But the sculptor's hand was steady and his vision true, and the immense lion that took shape beneath the cloth was a thing of grandeur. The lion sat, wings folded against its back, tail wrapped around its left side. From its smooth heavy haunches, to the muscles that rippled in its shoulders, to the sober gaze with which it measured the world, the lion seemed to emanate the power that had been promised. Even Cub, who had watched it emerge, stroke by stroke, from the shapeless mounds, couldn't help but feel sometimes that there was a *real* lion, just under the surface, watching and waiting.

The village children would peek in the windows, eyes just above the sill, and then bolt if the sculptor caught sight of them. Adults who came to the door with food or supplies peered into the dim interior, but never dared cross the threshold. They plied Cub with questions when he left the meeting hall on an errand, but, fearing for his leg, he was as taciturn as his master.

Even so, the gossip in the village centered on the sculpture – everyone talked about the lion and only about the lion. Their excitement dimmed, however, when Cub sent out the word that they would need to provide bronze for casting. The villagers grumbled, as implements and utensils, vessels and decorations that they had cherished went into bags to be melted down. They complained, yet each family put in what they could, and it was enough.

The time came that the lion was complete. Now the sculpture must be transformed into a mold for molten bronze. Stones were stacked in the square, creating kiln, furnace and steps, all that was needed for the process. Tinder and kindling and great split logs were stacked for fuel. Sand was brought from the river. Tallow and wax were gathered from every home. Only then was a team of village men allowed into the meeting house, where they fastened ropes to the platform beneath the mammoth lion, straining together to drag it into the square. There, in the twilight, the winged sculpture was unveiled before all the village, who marveled in hushed whispers at the lion's beauty.

The sculptor stood beside his creation, absorbing their awe with a look of distant amusement. Well could he afford to look amused, for he had a plan that served no one's ends but his own. The villagers had been right about the man's greed. Cub had been right that the man enjoyed the fear he inspired in others. And the midwife had been right about the darkness of the man's soul, because it was dark indeed, as black as pitch. Presently, the lion was covered again, and they all went home to sleep, so that the making of the mold could begin early in the morning. The rest of the process would take many hands. Only Cub, as was his habit, curled up on his mat beside the lion.

Cub awoke the next morning with the first rays of the dawn. In the last phases of the sculpting, the boy had been allowed to work on the lion himself, cleaning any crumbs of clay left by the tools of the sculptor, or any small lumps that may have fallen and adhered to the lower parts while the sculptor was working on the head and back. Now, as he lay looking at the massive shape beside him, Cub saw something he had missed. A rolled strand of clay had fallen on one of the lion's front paws and stuck there. He reached over and snapped it off, and then realized to his horror that the clay piece was scored on the back side and had been put there deliberately, that it was not a strand but a band, and that the band ran around the top of the lion's paw like a bracelet.

Cub was terrified, certain of the sculptor's wrath! He scrambled to his feet and stood trembling, looking at the broken band of clay in his hand. Then he ran to the well, lurching, and drew out a bucket of water. He picked up a metal cup that hung there for whoever might be thirsty, scooped out some water, and then holding it as steady as he could with his trembling hand and his limping gait, he carried the cup of water back to the lion. Dipping his fingers into the water, Cub rubbed the broken piece of clay and the ring of scratches on the lion, hoping to soften the clay for reworking. He pressed the broken band to the lion's paw, but the piece fell off. He tried again. It fell off again. He tried a third time. Finally, to his relief, the water dissolved the surface of the clay enough that the two parts stuck together. Cub sat back and sucked in a big gulp of air, and only then did his eyes fill with tears. He rubbed his face with his hand, smearing smudges of clay across his cheeks, and then he gently wiped the little drips of water that had fallen on the lion's paw. "I'm sorry," he whispered, and he went to return the cup.

The people arrived early that morning to commence work. When the sculptor appeared, Cub and the lion were surrounded already by the buzzing crowd. Cub began trembling again, wondering if the sculptor would notice the repaired paw, but the man merely glanced at him and said, "Go wash yourself. You look like you have been sleeping in mud." Then he turned to the people and began giving instructions.

They worked hard that day, and the next, and for many days thereafter. The sculptor directed the details and the people provided the labor. The smith, who knew fire and metal, worked hardest of all. At last a great bronze statue stood before them in the square. The winged lion shimmered in the pale rose light of the early morning.

With the awe-struck villagers gathered around, the sculptor drew from his pocket a small leather satchel bound with twine. He muttered low words in an ancient tongue, shook the contents of the sack over the lion's body and head, and then declared in a loud stern voice, "You are called to life as a guardian!"

Immediately, muscles flexed along the lion's side, bronze fur ruffled in the morning breeze, and the enormous wings shifted. Then, the lion blinked two amber eyes and slowly turned its head to look at the sculptor. He stepped in front of the now living statue and continued his spell.

"You exist to protect the people of this village. You will stay with them for all your years, as long as they and their children's children may live here in this valley." Then he turned to the people. "Behold your guardian. This lion will protect you from any living being that threatens you harm: from bears that eat your crops, cougars that snatch your children, disease that consumes your newborns and your elderly, and thieves who raid your sanctuary. But ..." and he gave a low laugh, "it will do so only upon *my* command. I will, of course, instruct the lion to save you, but only if you pay me for this additional service."

"That is unjust," protested one of the elders. "You spoke of no additional fee before. We paid as you required. That should be enough. Besides, we can ill afford to pay you more, when we already have given all that we have."

The sculptor simply shrugged. "The amount paid so far only covers my fee for creating the lion, not the lion's protection." He continued, "Since the guardian only obeys my wishes, I think when your need is great enough you will find the means to pay."

As he spoke, the sculptor glanced down to look at the band that encircled the lion's paw – the band linking the power of the lion to the man's will. But it was gone ... for when the lion had come to life, the broken pieces no longer adhered and had fallen away.

The man froze. His eyes narrowed and his face turned purple with rage. Cub, who had followed the man's gaze, gave a small frightened whimper and, stumbling backward, fell against the person behind him. "You!" screamed the man. He leaped forward to grab the boy, but the lion was faster. It pounced, and with a beating of gargantuan wings, the lion rose into the air with the sculptor clutched between its jaws.

As the lion flew away, objects fell from the sculptor's pockets – strange packets the people had never seen before, but also the coins and jewels they had gathered together to pay him for his work. High it climbed above the village, till the people could barely make out the form of the man between its teeth. Then, the lion slowly disappeared from their sight as well.

After a few minutes, a calm settled over the people, the first moment of peace they had experienced since the sculptor arrived in their village. They started to gather the fallen objects and return each to its rightful owner. The unknown packets were given to the midwife for inspection and safekeeping. Then they listened, over and over again, as Cub told the story of finding the band and breaking it off, and they realized how close they had come to bondage.

The next morning when they awoke, the villagers were surprised to discover the winged lion perched atop the meeting house, wings folded, looking for all the world like a statue of bronze. And there the lion stayed.

Through the coming years and the successive generations, the lion sat perched on the meeting house roof, and the villagers, though they struggled with nature's hardships, were free of the predations of any living creature, from man to the smallest inhabitant of the soil or air. And the story was passed down, from father to son and mother to daughter, of Cub, the boy who had saved their village from an evil magician who would have enslaved them with their own fear.

The Baker's Assistant

Once there was a girl, orphaned young, who worked as an assistant to the baker in a mountain village. She was not an apprentice, for in those times, a woman could not follow in the profession of a man, and baking was such a profession. As an assistant, she tended the ovens, stoking them to the right temperature and painstakingly spreading the coals so that the loaves would brown evenly. In the afternoon, when the day's baking was done, she cleaned the long wooden counters where the bread was kneaded and left for rising. She shoveled the ashes that had accumulated below the ovens, she swept and wiped, and, finally, when all was clean to the baker's satisfaction, she carried water from the river, jug after jug balanced on her head, and filled the square stone tank from which the baker would draw in the morning.

The work was not painful, nor was it satisfying. For years, she performed her tasks as many do, with occasional flashes of resentment and rarer moments of genuine pleasure. The baker was a solemn man of few words. Nearly deaf, yet denying any disability, he insisted that conversation was frivolous, and he resented intrusions into his realm of silence. As a consequence, the two worked in solitude, with a bond of mutual respect but little affection.

One afternoon in late summer, the girl lingered at the water's edge, her jug beside her, and watched a dry leaf turning on the current. A glint beneath the water caught her eye. Gathering her skirts in one arm and wading gingerly into the sharp, cold flow, she felt the river bottom and found a golden band as wide as her thumb and just large enough to slip over her hand and around her wrist. The band was etched with images and characters that undulated over the surface, and she knew that it must be both valuable and old.

Returning to shore, she tucked it deep into her pocket and, uncertain what else to do, finished her chore of filling the tank. Back and forth between the river and the bakery she walked, the jug heavy on her head, then empty, then heavy, then empty. But she scarcely noticed, for her mind was only on the mystery in her pocket. For the first time in her life, she wished desperately that she could read.

That night, in her small room at the back of the bakery, she lay in bed turning the golden band in her hands, tracing the patterning with her fingers. When she woke, she took time in the dim light of the predawn to fumble through her chest of possessions till she found a needle and a length of coarse wool. This she stitched in the bottom of the pocket so she could tie the band there.

All that day, her step was light and her look was far away, so that the baker eyed her sharply, wondering if she had fallen in love. Having spent so many years in silence, the girl had developed an ample imagination, full of people and places and dreams. Now the seeds of her quiet yearnings were watered by hope, and they began to grow. Perhaps, she thought, this band is magic. Perhaps it is a band of power. Perhaps I can fly wherever my imaginings can carry me. Perhaps it holds the means to change things or people or situations. Perhaps it is changing me even now, as it lies in my pocket.

That night, she said to the baker with a tone of resolve that he had never before heard, "I want to learn to read."

"You have no time," he said. "In all these years it has taken the whole day long for you to complete your tasks and for me to complete mine. I need you here, not toying with some foolishness. Besides, you are female. Have you forgotten? What use has a woman of your standing for such a skill?"

But she persisted. "You know I am old enough to marry now and make my own decisions, to leave this position that you gave me when you took me from the orphanage. I am not ungrateful, but I am grown. If I married, you would have no assistant at all, and it would be a long time before any new orphan child could complete these tasks with my ease and efficiency. Yet I am not asking to marry. I am asking for time to study. I am willing to rise earlier and to work later, to tend this bakery. But I want to learn."

"You will look the fool, in among children and the daughters of the wealthy," said the baker. But he was thinking about how difficult it was for him to hear, and how much communication would be required to train a new assistant. And his protest fell weakly against the wall of her resolve. So it was done.

She did look foolish sitting in the back of the classroom, a grown woman in a shabby dress towering above the rows of boys. They stared at her. The well-dressed daughters of merchants buzzed among themselves, dismayed, for their own presence in the school was a sign of status – a gesture which showed their families had surplus to spend conferring on their daughters skills that would never be used for anything other than parlor conversation.

But the baker's assistant was not dissuaded. She paid the reluctant teacher out of coppers she had carefully hoarded over the years, and she attended the school tenaciously through the winter, fighting her way to the classroom through blowing snow and biting wind. She would rise in the dead of night so that the bakery would be ready to open, stumbling in the dark over slippery cobblestones to carry her jug from the black river with its skim of ice.

Always, she carried with her the secret band, convinced more than ever of its power. Had not the baker bowed his will before her? Had not the teacher grudgingly and then warmly supported her presence in the classroom? Hadn't the boys with their initial profusion of sharp twigs and annoying pebbles and jostling elbows now accepted her like some exotic foreigner in the back of their class? They felt the band's power, just as she could feel its hard curve against her leg. Now, they turned to her with their questions and gave her offerings of dried meat and fruit in return for her knowledge. *If it helps me this much now,* she thought, *how far will I be able to reach when I really know how to use it?*

She was a sharp student, and serious. By early spring she could write simple sentences on a slate, or read aloud slowly from the teacher's cherished books. By the time the snows melted, she had read and reread all his books and began to wrestle, instead, with numbers and coaching some of the younger students through their assignments.

It was that spring that she realized the symbols on the band were not written in her own language. When she studied the inscription under the flicker of her candle, the characters danced, familiar yet unfamiliar, teasingly similar to the script she knew so well, yet indecipherable. *Perhaps,* she thought, *they are an ancient tongue, or perhaps a tongue known only to mages and sorcerers and healers.*

When the planting season started, the school doors closed for the summer. On the last day of class, the baker's assistant went to thank the teacher and to take her leave.

"Wait," he said. "I have something to give you." From his desk he took a slender book of parchment bound in leather. "This was given to me many years ago by an elderly man, who said that I would know when it was time to pass it on. In all my years, I have never met anyone with your hunger for learning. The time has come." He placed the worn volume in her hands.

She looked at him in surprised silence, then opened to the first page. "From our Mother with the rising sun …" she read aloud, in the words of an ancient liturgy. Then her eyes blurred with tears, and she could read no more. "Thank you," she said, overcome with emotion, and as the teacher watched she fled out the door.

That night she curled in her room, blanketed in more contentment than she had ever known. By candle light she traced letters in the precious book: "On high flow the waters, in the depths rise the springs, from the soul …" Later, she dreamt herself a young girl on a windy hill, kneeling at the grave of the parents she had lost. And the wind wrapped the words of the liturgy around her, healing a wound she had not known she carried.

She awoke, more sure than ever of herself and her quest. When the baking was done and the sun glinted above the rooftops, slanting in through the window onto a mound of fresh brown bread, she slipped out the door and went to see the herbalist.

"I am here to offer myself as an apprentice," she said simply. The herbalist, who was bent over a formula, straightened his back, groaning slightly at the movement. He peered through age-blurred eyes at the determined young woman who stood before him, poised and certain, waiting. It was a long time since he had thought about seeking an apprentice. He had thought the time had come and gone. And yet here she stood, looking immovable. His eyes creased slightly at the corners. "I thought you would never come," he said.

So the baker's assistant became the herbalist's apprentice. Out of loyalty, she continued her labor in the bakery, but most of her time was now spent grinding and mixing herbs. She learned seasonings and spices, she learned remedies and potions. And as the eyes of the herbalist slowly failed, she read aloud to him formulas and charms, rituals and lore that had been painstakingly documented by his predecessors. When business was slow, she would take a pen and record, as he had done in his youth, the legacy of knowledge that was being entrusted to her.

Two years passed this way. In the second spring, the baker came to her. "I have heard that in the valley a young baker's apprentice seeks a position. I would like to send for him and have him join me. He could take over the tasks you are doing as well as learn my trade. It seems your life calls you elsewhere."

"Yes," she responded with gratitude, thinking that the band was guiding her destiny.

The baker hesitated. "I thought you a fool, wasting your coppers on reading. But I was wrong. Go now with my blessing." Into her hand he pressed a small sack of coins to replace those she had spent on her education.

That afternoon, she packed her possessions tightly into her trunk. With a small gesture of leave-taking, she touched the bed and chair that had been her home since childhood.

As she departed, she thanked the baker again for his kindness. Then she moved into a sparse room above the herbalist's shop.

Thereafter, she devoted herself entirely to her apprentice tasks, working side by side with the older man. Gradually, her responsibilities grew and his diminished, until it came to be that he rested in a chair by the street in the summer and by the fire in the winter, and she was no longer called the herbalist's apprentice, but simply the herbalist. She listened carefully to the people who came seeking healing, and as time went on, they increasingly sought from her not only herbs but also advice.

Travelers came to her shop, not just midwives and physicians, but also those who were reputed to know the older, darker arts. As her reputation grew, people came seeking consultation about medicines and surgical procedures, sharing rituals of more advanced trades. "Knowledge I trade for knowledge," she would say. "I will tell you what I can, but you must teach me in return." Then she would cease her grinding, measuring, and mixing and brew dark strong tea, sitting with her guests by the fire for as long as they needed in order to hear and be heard.

Still, the mystery of the band was not forgotten. She made a rubbing with coal on parchment of the figures etched in the gold. When the time seemed right, she would show the parchment to guests and ask whether they could read the script. But all shook their heads. "Perhaps in the Great Library on the coast," they would say. "Perhaps the keepers can read these words." But the coast was far away, and the need around her great. Her competence bound her to the herbal shop, as it had once bound her to the bakery. The village needed her.

One day she looked up to find a messenger from the Royal City standing in her door. "The king's child is dying," he said. "Messengers have been sent throughout the land to seek the greatest healers. You are counted among them."

"You honor me beyond merit," she said humbly. "Surely there are others much wiser than I in the Royal City." But the man stood firm. So she tidied the shop, sealed away her wares, and made arrangements with a neighbor to tend the elderly herbalist. She packed a bag for the trip. In it she placed her small sack of coins, rare herbs bound gently in cloth, and the book from the teacher. The band, of course, was packed as well.

When she arrived in the palace compound, she was taken straight away to the sickroom. The doctors conferred in hasty mutterings outside the door, telling her what they knew. "I would prefer to go in alone," she said with a slight nervousness.

The room was shuttered and dim. An ornate bed stood alone in the center. From it, a thin waif of a girl, pale and fragile and with dark hair and large blue eyes, looked up at her with neither fear nor expectation. Many had come and gone from this room before, and the child knew she was dying. The woman stood for a moment getting her bearings, then set down her bag and did what she did best: she listened. She listened to the child's halting words. She listened to her chest and abdomen. She listened to the room itself. Then she felt the girl's forehead, the pulse in her arm, and the beating of the small heart beneath the ribs. Mostly though, she listened to her own body, knowing that the power of the band flowed through it.

"Rest," she said to the child. "Rest and I will tell you what I know." So the child closed her eyes and the woman drew from her bag the small book and began reading softly, "In the spring come the rains. The earth softens to receive them. Heavy grows the rich dark soil, heavy with beginnings …" Gradually, the ancient text soothed the child, and she understood somehow that the woman was healing her with these written words. Peace penetrated her hopelessness, and she drifted off to sleep.

"What did you find?" asked the doctors when the woman left the room.

"I will speak only to the king," she answered.

They stared at her surprised. "You can't do that. We called for you. We hold the authority to tend this child. The king cannot be bothered with the guesses and attempted ministrations of every healer who passes through this room."

"Nevertheless, call the king. Tell him I will speak to him in a room with his advisors and his family, all who care for the child. Only then will I share what I have learned."

The king was angered at her audacity but also intrigued, and he loved his daughter. He left his work in the tribunal and called for a gathering in the great hall. When all had arrived, he turned to the woman. "What do you have to say?" he asked sternly.

The woman met his gaze. "Your child is being poisoned."

A hushed gasp ran through the room. "Are you certain?" asked the king. "How do you know?"

"It is a power I have, a power I carry."

"Would you stake your life on it?"

"I think," she replied, "that I just did." He nodded in assent. She turned to the assembled company who stood frozen before her. As they watched, she studied them carefully, one by one, waiting for each to meet her eyes before moving on. She finished, then began studying them again. Midway through the crowd, her scrutiny came to rest on a tall man with a hawk's gray eyes and a hard, thin mouth. "Why don't you tell them?" she prompted quietly.

"I don't know what you mean," he said curtly. But he did, and when the others looked at him, they could sense his duplicity too. The man turned toward the king hoping for mercy. Without a word, the king motioned for the guards, and he was led away.

"There are others here who also bear you and your family ill will," said the woman. "But they are weaker. If you allow them to leave, I think they will be gone by morning."

Time seemed to stand still. "So let it be," said the king finally. "With death awaiting, if they should ever be found again in the Royal City."

That night, the former baker's assistant dined with the royal family. "I never thought," said the king, "that my cousin's envy would grow so great that it would consume him. That he would poison a child, *my* child."

"The poison came from his soul," she responded. "He may have bought it with his gold and ground it with his hands, but it came from his soul. Why did he hate you so?"

The king sighed and brushed his forehead with his hand. "Seven years ago, the Council of Elders changed a law. No longer, they said, could a woman be barred from a man's position – including that of king. Under the old law of succession, my cousin was heir to my throne, because my wife died giving birth to our daughter and females were barred from ruling. My cousin fought the new law but lost. Now, due to your skill, he has lost again, this time his life, though I find no joy in it." He lapsed into a distant silence, and then, after several minutes, returned. "But I do find joy, joy without measure, in knowing that my daughter is nearly healed, that she will grow and play and sing again! Truly, I am indebted. Is there anything I can do for you?"

"One thing," replied the woman. She drew from her pocket the band of gold and set it on the table. "I should like to know the meaning of this inscription."

The king laughed. "Is that all?"

"That is all," she said. "Otherwise, I have everything I need, and more."

The next morning the woman was escorted to the Great Library. She stood awestruck among the hundreds of volumes that contained the experience and wisdom of her people. One by one the keepers were called to see if they could decipher the script. Finally one came, stooped and gray, a master of forgotten languages. "Yes," he said, "I can read it." He turned the band slowly in his hand several times and then began to speak:

I am born of earth and sky,
With roots that thread through shattered stone.
Between fire and ice,
Between the mountain of the rising sun and the sea,
One I am with them, and
Many they in me.

"Is there more?" she said.

"Is there more?" he chuckled. "That is a lot to fit on a simple band of gold."

"But is there an incantation? An oath? A ritual …?" she trailed off, not knowing what else to ask.

He looked at her, confused. "It is a poem," he said. "A celebration of life, of living." He handed the band back to her.

She turned it in her hand, staring at the forms that were so familiar she could see them with her eyes shut. "A celebration of life," she repeated, dazed. Then she laughed. "Yes," she said, "I see that it is. Thank you so much."

"Did you find what you sought?" asked the king when she returned to the palace.

"Yes," she answered, "I am ready to return to my home."

"I will send you with horses," he said, "and a guard." But she declined, preferring to walk.

On the way out of the Royal City, the healer asked directions and made one stop, at an orphanage. "I seek an apprentice," she told the director. They showed her a girl, ten or twelve, with pale skin and pale eyes that had seen too much. "Will you come with me?" asked the woman, and the girl agreed.

They walked together in silence till they came to a bridge outside the city gate. There the woman stopped, staring down into the glistening waters. Again, she laughed. "Come," she said to the red-headed child, and she drew her to the center of the bridge. Kneeling, she took from her bag a length of emerald green ribbon, and from her pocket the band of gold. She threaded the band onto the ribbon, and then she tied it as a necklace around the white throat of the wide-eyed child.

"This band has magical powers," she said. "It has the power to alter situations and inspire people to be their best selves. If you look and listen carefully, you will see things you never noticed before. It also has the power to heal. Perhaps, it is changing you even now, helping you to grow and blossom in wondrous ways."

Then the woman lifted her bag onto her back and took the girl's hand. They continued on their journey, over the bridge and upward toward the mountains.

Deas

Once there was a girl, an only child named Ryah, who lived in a bustling town nestled between two mountains. One peak they called the Mountain of the Sun, for the sun peered over its shoulder each morning to light the spires and then the rooftops and then the cobblestones of the town. The other they called the Mountain of the Witch, for an ancient witch lived there, high in the crags, in a crumbling fortress made of dark stone.

Ryah was a quiet child, happy, but different from the others. When she wasn't in school or helping her mother, Renn, with the house or garden, she liked to wander or sit by herself, creating little things her people called "deas." She made them out of almost anything – clay or stone or leaves, scraps of fabric, broken sticks – sometimes out of nothing at all. With her hands she would build and shape her creations and then arrange them around her and admire them with the pleasure of a satisfied artist. And then, because her world was different than this one, she would watch as the deas began to float above the ground and glow, each with its own hue.

Sometimes, Ryah left the deas of clay lying where she made them, glowing faintly. Or sometimes she carried them home and stashed them around the basins and cistern and beneath the hanging clothes that filled the small courtyard behind her home. There they would drift in the air until forgotten. Eventually, their light would fade or they would dissolve in the rain, or Renn, impatient with the abandoned accumulation, would clear them away with her broom.

When Ryah's hands were busy or when she had none of her favorite materials nearby to work with (like while she hung clothes or weeded the garden or lay in bed at night), she invented deas in her mind. Her imagination provided all the resources she needed. The deas Ryah created in her imagination appeared as glowing spheres that hung in the air around her shoulders, trailing lazily behind her as she moved from place to place. Each held faintly in its center the image that had formed itself in her mind. Misty and thin at first, they would grow more sharp and solid the more she thought about them. Once created, they would drift and bump into each other, sometimes changing form and color before they disappeared. Occasionally, one would become so solid that Ryah could actually pluck it out of the air and put it into her pocket. But that took an awful lot of thinking about one thing.

Sooner or later, though, they all disappeared, for Ryah's creations, like those of most children, were spontaneous and brief. She delighted in them, but made no attempt to hold on to them. Some glowed for a day or more, tucked into her pocket or clustered in the courtyard or drifting by her shoulder, but her attention flitted from discovery to discovery, and sooner or later each one faded away.

The neighbors looked with suspicion on the deas that glimmered around Ryah as she walked to school or did her errands or played in the fields around the town. It's not that Ryah was the only child who could make deas. The other children were sometimes trailed by a dea or two or even three – just never a whole flock of them like Ryah. Instead, the other children spent most of their time on chores and games and squabbles. "She's an odd one, leave her be," parents told their sons and daughters. They meant, stay away from her. And the children did.

"Daft," muttered the gossips in the market, who marked the ground with protective hexes after Ryah and Renn left their stalls, their bags laden with earthy vegetables, a faint scatter of glowing deas trailing along behind them.

"Not daft!" whispered Renn under her breath. "But she is just like her father, Arn." However, Renn did not say this to the women in the market. She couldn't tell them that night after night her husband came home from his carpentry, ate dinner and then, while she sat with her knitting and Ryah her books, he would disappear into the small nook that held his desk. There he sat for hours by candlelight, thinking, drawing on scraps of paper, and scratching out the designs that had played in his imagination all day as he worked. When, finally, the candle burned low or weariness overtook him, Arn would wad the papers into small brown lumps, hard and tight, and he would lock them into the drawers beneath his desk.

One afternoon, as Ryah helped to prepare the evening meal, she asked, "Mother, why does father crush all of his deas into little clumps and lock them away?"

Renn looked startled. "Why do you think they are deas?" she asked.

"Because they are," said Ryah. "And if he let them go free they would glow."

Renn was silent for a long moment. "Yes," she said finally. "They would. But it's not allowed."

"What do you mean, not allowed?" said Ryah. "*My* deas are allowed."

"Only because you are a child," said her mother, "and you see how people treat you. Someday you too will need to keep your deas from shining and hovering around your shoulders and following you through the town."

"But why?" asked Ryah again, "I like them."

Renn hesitated. Then she set down her knife and the yam she had been slicing, and she put on her storytelling voice. "A long time ago," she said, "in the days of my grandmother's grandmother, the people of our town used to make deas whenever they had the urge. Young and old, male and female, they wrote them or drew them or sculpted them like you do, or simply imagined them and set them loose. The deas floated in the air and underfoot. They bumped into each other and changed color and shape, those from one person merging with those from another.

"If one of the floating deas caught someone's fancy, it attached itself to that person and trailed behind him or her, bumping into other deas so that new ones formed. Over time, if a person liked and paid attention and thought about them enough, the deas became solid. Not just easier to see. You could touch them or hold them or change them with your hands or tools as well as your mind."

"Mine do that!" interrupted Ryah.

"Yes," said her mother. "You could make things out of them if you wanted to, and that is what people did. They would pluck their very best deas out of the air and put them someplace to continue shaping them, someplace like a workshop or a studio or a special corner just for deas, like your father's desk.

"Over time, people learned how to turn their deas into elaborate creations: pictures and sculptures and music, anything you might imagine. Some objects that were especially delightful became art to decorate the town square and the shrines, the library, museum, and people's homes. Some deas that were particularly useful developed into tools that the villagers used in their day-to-day work of blacksmithing or sewing or planting or keeping accounts. People saved the tools made from deas and began to copy them, which made their work even easier.

"But not all deas were beautiful or useful. Some were ugly or strange or dark, even some that came from goodhearted people."

"I have dark deas sometimes," confessed Ryah.

Her mother nodded sympathetically, remembering the glowing gray flock that had followed her daughter after a particularly bad day of teasing. "I have noticed. But dark deas fade away, unless we focus on them and cultivate them and keep them alive. The problem in the old days started because sometimes a dark dea *did* appeal to someone who, over time, turned it into something ugly and real. My grandmother, who told me the story, said that such deas appealed to the darkness in the villagers themselves – their jealousies, resentments, or sorrows that refused healing. When that happened, the dark deas stayed and grew and became more solid. And they could become quite monstrous: art that inspired cruelty rather than compassion, tools that became weapons for destroying rather than building, and hideous deformed images that left our people feeling haunted and troubled, that brought them bad dreams . . . or worse.

"So the villagers both loved the deas and feared them, and in this mix of love and fear a shrewd man saw an opportunity. He was mayor of our town, a wealthy merchant who had made his money, some said, through stinginess and questionable trades. Still, there were those who overlooked his methods and admired his success. He had fancy parties and courted the favor of those in power, and once he even persuaded nobles from the Royal City to visit our town and stay in his house. So, when it came time to seek a mayor, his influence gained him the position.

"Now the mayor was irritated by deas – by their unruliness, by their unpredictability, by the fact that their owners could not control them. His irritation gradually grew into a determination that he *would* find a way to control them … and a way to own them. First, he tried capturing deas and boxing them. But boxed, they simply disappeared and returned to whoever was interested in them, where they continued evolving as before.

"Frustrated, the mayor began to consort with those who know magic – not healers or sages, for the lightworkers would have nothing to do with his quest – but with practitioners of the dark arts, both human and not. Eventually, he found what he wanted.

"One day he gathered the town council together and held up a jar. In it was a small object; nobody recalls exactly what. Perhaps it was a curious little carving or piece of unusual jewelry. Maybe it was something practical like a fastener or awl, but slightly different than the ones the people already used. 'What is it?' the council members asked.

"'It is a dea,' he answered, '*made valuable.*' He took it out of the jar and exclaimed, 'Look – it doesn't change or disappear! It stays where you want it to stay and does what you want it to do. It can be stored for long periods of time and carted over great distances. And, most importantly, it can be bought and sold and traded.'

"Then, he picked up a second, larger canister and held it high for all of them to see. He continued, 'With this magic powder, deas can be changed into pods we can control. There is a man who will buy deas from us for money and turn them into pods. He will then sell them back to those who wish, tamed and transformed.'

"At first, the town council resisted, for they did not understand why anyone would want to capture and bind the deas into pods. The mayor ignored them. Instead, he appealed to the greed of the merchants, who started to see an opportunity for profit. Then he appealed to the pride of craftsmen, who saw how the objects they fabricated could no longer be easily copied with new deas. And he appealed to the envy of those who had difficulty producing deas, and to the shame of those who accidentally produced dark ones. In short, he appealed to the basest of human urgings, our darkest cravings and deepest fears.

"Eventually, the town council agreed with the mayor's pod proposal, and a law was passed forbidding deas in our town, save in the form of the pods. Moreover, all involved in the storage and trading of deas were required to have permits and pay taxes, which in turn paid for the enforcement of the new law.

Soon, shops sprang up where people were forced to sell their banned deas. And an odd-looking peddler – half human, some said, or a troll – began arriving weekly in town. The merchants gave him the deas which he turned into pods. Some pods he took to do business in other towns, and some he converted into objects and gave back to the merchants to sell here.

"To this day, our deas are bought and sold in this manner, transformed into pods for safekeeping, and then converted into items for sale. As a result, the mayor became vastly wealthy, as have all mayors who came after him and a few of our merchants. It is said that deas are bought and sold in other towns as well, but nowhere are deas as beautiful and as bountiful as here."

At the word "bountiful," Renn met her daughter's eyes and stopped talking. She then smiled a wry smile, glanced toward her husband's nook, and picked up her knife and began slicing again.

Ryah noticed her mother's grim look and cautiously asked, "But what about father? Does he sell his deas?"

"No, though he breaks the law by refusing," said Renn. "Yet, he can't stop making them."

"I don't understand," said Ryah, with confused thoughts swimming in her head.

Her mother explained more slowly, "Your father believes that selling deas is wrong, that deas should be allowed to go free, that they belong to no one and to everyone. Arn also believes that the shapes the deas could grow into if allowed to mingle freely would be far more wonderful than the objects made from the pods. Do you understand now?"

Ryah shook her head in disbelief. "I thought all the things in the shops were made by our townspeople or made by people in faraway towns and villages."

"Finish your work," said her mother with a sadness in her voice. "Tomorrow I will explain further. You are old enough now to know the truth."

Later that night while she washed the dinner plates, Ryah noticed for the first time a small dish of powder that her father kept on his desk. She watched him as he dipped his fingers into the dish and sprinkled a black substance over his crumpled design – what she now realized was a dea pod.

The following day when they went to the market, Renn took her daughter into a shop that Ryah had never visited before. Handsome panels of embroidery hung on a rack in one corner and small tools lay on a shelf. Renn gestured toward rows of jars that lined one wall, each containing some intriguing object. The items were curious and beautiful. An old shopkeeper scowled at the deas that hovered around Ryah's shoulders. "What do you want?" he asked gruffly.

"We'll know when we find it," answered Renn. She waited quietly while her daughter surveyed the shelves. Ryah looked from one object to another, then she turned abruptly and walked out the door. "What we seek is not here," said Renn, and she followed her daughter out into sunlight.

Outside, Ryah was silent. "They are dead," she said finally. "Like those snakes and baby animals in jars at the shop of old Fernem, the healer. They are interesting, but they are dead." She wiped at tears that smarted in the corners of her eyes. Her mother put a hand on her shoulder, and they walked home in silence.

For a long while after that, Ryah noticed that many of her own deas were odd or dark or half-formed. After she finished chores and schoolwork, she would begin to play with whatever lay in her hands or in her mind. But then the memory of the shop would come crowding in, and she would imagine her deas preserved in jars and she could not finish molding them. As seasons passed, she dreaded the time when she would be old enough that her deas, like her father's, must be hidden. Hidden or sold.

Aware of the law, she found herself spending her free time playing more and more in the fields and forest that encircled the village, away from the disapproval of her human companions. By a stream that flowed from the Mountain of the Sun, she found a glade where she could be alone, a quiet place full of humming bees and the steamy scent of wild herbs. There she felt free, and once again her hands could make shapes or her imagination could conjure images that she found delightful and satisfying.

One day in the middle of summer, Ryah began scooping clay from the stream bank and shaping it into creatures that made her laugh. Caught up in her project, she passed the entire afternoon oblivious to her surroundings, completely absorbed in her work until the cry of a crow broke her trance.

Ryah looked up at him. How long had he been sitting on the ground beside her? He cocked his head to one side and cawed again. "Are you laughing at my creatures, too?" asked Ryah. The crow bobbed his head, as if to agree. Ryah stared at him, surprised. But then, as she stared, she realized how late it was becoming and that her mother must be preparing dinner alone. Leaving her creatures where they lay, she jumped to her feet and began to splash, washing her hands in the stream. The crow, startled, flew away.

Ryah trotted back to the village, thinking about the crow. "It was almost like he understood me," she told her parents over dinner.

"Crows are like that," said Arn. "They know more than some humans."

The next day, Ryah hurried back to the glade, still thinking about the crow and wondering if she would see him again. But when she reached the clearing, all thought of the bird vanished from her mind. There on the creek bank stood the creatures she had made the day before, but scattered among them were others, as peculiar and funny as her own.

Ryah touched them and then looked around. "Who has been here?" she asked aloud. An answering caw came from a branch above her. "Was it you?" Ryah asked the crow. "Did you make these incredible creatures?" The crow just cocked his head to one side and looked mischievous. "You know, don't you?" said Ryah, laughing. "Tell me. Who made them?"

"I did," said a husky voice from the woods on the other side of the clearing. Out of the trees stepped a person like none Ryah had ever seen before. He was about as tall as she was but twice as wide. His head was large, with a lumpy nose and wild hair sticking out in all directions. Wide hairy feet stuck out of shabby pants, and in one hand he held a bucket of clay. He was ugly enough that Ryah might have been frightened, but because of the plants and the creatures and the place, she wasn't.

"What *are* you?" asked Ryah, and then, thinking it a rude question, she hastily added, "I mean *who* are you?"

The person chuckled and said, "I'm Merly, to answer your second question. To answer your first, a troll. A bit more than half-grown." He looked her over. "I guess that makes me 'bout as old for a troll as you are for a human." He moved over to the clay creatures and began touching them. "Do you like my animals? Watch this." To Ryah's amazement, they began to move, some swaying or bending, others moving their arms, a couple taking funny steps. She watched as the creatures moved about for several minutes and then gradually stopped.

"Fantastic!" she exclaimed, when the creatures had all frozen into new positions. "How can you do that?"

Merly shrugged. "Trolls is trolls," he said. "There's things we can't do and things we can. Most trolls aren't interested in making things or animatin' them, unless it's fer to scare off bothersome humans or to chase down animals fer eatin'. But I think it's fun. I like makin' things just to make 'em." He pointed to a couple of faint deas that hovered around Ryah's shoulders. "How can you do that?"

"We call them deas," said Ryah. "I just think of them and they appear."

"Mine are deas too," said Merly. "But I don't have those kind."

While they were talking, the crow flew down and landed on Merly's shoulder. "Hi Trey," said Merly, "are you wantin' some attention?"

"Do you know him?" asked Ryah.

"Of course," said Merly. He lifted up his arm so that the crow hopped onto his wrist, then he held the bird out to Ryah. Intrigued, Ryah stepped closer and held out her own arm, and the crow hopped from Merly to her. "Trey is my familiar," said Merly. "Where's yours?"

"What do you mean?" asked Ryah. "I don't think I have one." She touched the crow gingerly.

"Everybody has a familiar!" insisted Merly. "Else who would be with you when you're alone? How would you find your way in the forest if you wander too far? Who would help you commun'cate with animals? Who helps you do your magic?"

"I don't have one," said Ryah firmly. "When I'm alone, I am alone. If I am lost I have to find my own way. And I don't do magic."

Merly looked dismayed. Then he brightened. "At least we both have deas," he said. "That's a kind of magic." He plunked his bucket of clay next to the creatures, which now stood still. "Here." He gestured to Ryah to join him and began scooping clay out of the bucket.

From that moment on, the two of them were fast friends. Whenever Ryah found time to slip away from her responsibilities, she went to the glade. And thanks to Trey's watchful eye, Merly usually arrived soon after. There, using the clay of the stream bank, the two of them created a whole village of fantastical creatures, with dwellings of all sizes and shapes, and machines that had no purpose other than to look complicated and peculiar. Every so often, Merly would animate all the creatures at the same time, and then the two of them would sit and point and laugh, especially the time a hard rain turned all of their clay creatures into odd lumps and Merly animated them anyway.

"What if someone else from the village finds this clearing?" Ryah lamented once.

Merly looked at her surprised. "Troll magic ain't the best, but who would ever leave their special place open to the public? I put confusin' spells on the path the very first time we met here, just like trolls do with their caves. Ain't you wondered why no deer ever been here to tromp our critters?"

Sometimes Ryah and Merly worked hard at their project and sometimes they mostly talked. They talked about humans who thought deas were only good if turned into pods for buying and selling. They talked about trolls, in particular those who thought everything worth making had already been made and that young ones should "leave well 'nough alone." They talked about what Ryah knew from her schooling and what Merly knew from the forest. They talked about how to ignore taunting and how to get even. They talked about faraway lands and secret places that were dear to them. They talked about their parents and about growing up and growing old. And they talked about magic, which was their favorite topic.

As the summer began winding into fall, Ryah and Merly stumbled upon a thicket of blackberries and discovered another thing they had in common. Merly loved his mother's blackberry-rodent stew, and Ryah loved her mother's blackberry-rhubarb pie. So they began to spend much of their time tromping through the woods to favorite meadows looking for blackberries. As often as not, Ryah would arrive home at the end of the day scratched and grubby, two buckets in each hand filled with all the berries she could possibly carry. Renn fretted about Ryah being off in the woods so much, but she could see that her daughter was as happy as she had ever been, and the pantry shelves were filling with canned berries for winter, so she let it be.

Although the days grew shorter, their excursions grew longer. One day Ryah picked berries till the shadows stretched long and the sun slipped behind the forested slopes across the valley. As she bent over the last tempting, scratchy bush, Trey returned from one of his jaunts and swooped onto the ground beside Merly with a loud caw.

Merly interpreted the crow's brooding look. "He's tellin' us that somethin's wrong."

"It's me," Ryah scowled, looking at the sky. "I've stayed too late. My parents warned me twice this week. Now I won't be allowed to come tomorrow."

Merly looked at the crow and opened his mouth to say something and then closed it again. "Maybe that's it," he said.

Ryah hurried back home, dreading the scolding that awaited her. But when she stepped inside the door, she knew immediately that something far worse was wrong. All around her, the family furniture stood askew. Her mother sat hunched at the table crying with her hands over her face. An upturned earthen bowl and cup lay broken on the floor beside her, along with a mess of stewed vegetables and milk. And her father's desk lay on its side, with his papers, quills and inkwell scattered across the floor.

"Mama!" Ryah cried. She dropped her buckets with a clatter by the door and stumbled to her mother's side. "What's wrong? What happened?" she begged, choking on fear.

Renn reached out an arm and pulled her close. "They took your father away. Maybe one of the neighbors told … Somehow, they found out about his deas. Most of them are still hidden, but they found enough to arrest him."

That night was worse than any Ryah had ever known. When she and Renn were able, they put the furniture back as best they could, and Ryah cleaned the broken things from the floor. "We have to get rid of the rest of the deas," Renn said. "They may search here again. If they knew how many there are …" In the larder she emptied apples out of a rough cotton bag that sat in the corner. Then she pried a stone from the floor by the desk. Beneath it was a hollow filled with pods. With trembling hands, she scooped the pods into the bag. "Where should I take them?" she asked, speaking more to herself than to Ryah.

"Let me take them," said Ryah. "Let me go. I know a place in the forest where no one ever comes, and I can find my way there in the dark. Besides, I'm still a child, and if they catch me, they will be much easier on me than you." Her mother protested but she didn't have a better plan, and in the end she had to agree. So, after the moon rose, the candles went out, and the dogs fell silent, Ryah slipped back through the streets and out across the field to the stream, which she followed into the darkness of the forest.

Beneath the cover of the trees she made her way, grateful for the dim glow of the deas that hovered about her shoulders. Finally, she came to the glade. There, in the dark mud at the creek's bank, she could barely make out the whimsical clay creatures she had last seen by daylight – back, it seemed, when the whole world was different. Hastily, Ryah untied the bag and scattered her father's pods across the ground, flinging out great handfuls, until at last the bag was empty. Then she fled back through the night.

When she reached home, Ryah crawled into bed with her mother. Renn hugged her in the dark. "Are they safe?" she whispered.

Ryah froze. *Are they safe?* "You said, 'Get rid of them', " she answered. *But of course! Her father had kept his deas buried for years. Why hadn't she thought to tuck the bag into a tree nook or under a rock instead of scattering them on the damp bank with her deas and Merly's …*

"I'm sorry," whispered Renn, feeling slightly anxious. "Don't worry about it. The most important thing was taking them away." But Ryah felt wretched as she fell into exhausted sleep. Somehow, perhaps she could regather the pods in the morning.

The following day, the children in the neighborhood were horrible. They taunted Ryah by calling Arn a criminal and saying she would become one too. The teens simply stared at her and gossiped quietly amongst themselves.

As soon as she knew that her mother was safe in the company of faithful friends, Ryah slipped away again, through the woods to the glade. When she got to the edge of the clearing, she stopped in astonishment.

In a broad arc across the glade, where she had scattered the pods in the dark, the ground had sprung up with curious and wondrous plants. Some barely poked out of the soil, some were as high as her knees, and all of them had pods clinging to their leaves. In addition, the clay creatures were moving, wiggling or waddling or walking on many legs or none at all.

"Merly?" she called. Trey answered first from the branches above her, then Merly stepped from behind a tree.

"These are great!" he said. "How'd you make so many?" Then he saw Ryah's face and he stopped.

Ryah choked out her story. When finished, she clenched her fists and cried, "I wish I could free all the deas! I want to throw away the black powder that turns them into pods! I want to break the bad magic that caused this law! And I want my father out of jail!"

Merly lowered his head. He picked up a stick and slowly broke it into small pieces. "I know somethin' about it … troll secret," he mumbled quietly.

Ryah wiped her wet, smudgy face. "What are you talking about?" she asked.

"I never told you 'cause the other trolls wouldn't like it. They might …" he winced and stopped. "They don't like trolls helpin' humans or givin' 'em information." He stopped again. Ryah waited. "The pods are taken to the Mountain of the Witch. I heard my parents say that a troll from the other side of the mountain helps her. He's the one who brings the powder to your town that turns deas into pods. Then he takes the pods to the witch. She makes 'em into what you call 'dead deas,' and the troll carries 'em back to town."

"My mother said it might be a troll!" exclaimed Ryah. "But she wasn't sure."

"He looks sorta human 'cause the witch gave him magic to disguise himself. But I don't think it works very well. I've never seen him myself, but some of my uncles were, well, spying by the market to see if there was any stuff worth takin'. They told my father that when the troll puts on his disguise, he doesn't look like anythin' you ever saw, not really human and not really troll. 'Vile and disgustin',' they said. 'Makes you want to vomit rat tails! Someone oughta teach him a lesson 'bout what trolls is spos'd to look like.' But they left him alone 'cause they're scared of that witch."

"Dark magic," said Ryah, now angry. "Of course!" She wiped her arm across her face. "I am going to the Mountain of the Witch," she announced.

"To the *witch*? You can't, Ryah! I shouldn'a told you! Who knows what she might do to you?" Merly said horrified. "Besides, you'll never find the way."

"I *will* find the way. We've been finding our way through the forest all month. I can find a big old fortress."

"But I can't go with you," pleaded Merly. "I've already said things that trolls aren't spos'd to say to humans."

"I am going," repeated Ryah. "And I will find the way."

Merly begged. But the more he tried to dissuade her, the more determined Ryah became. Finally he said, "Then I'll give you Trey to go with you." He reached out an arm and called for the bird, who flew to them and landed on Merly's wrist. Merly stroked his back. "Go with Ryah," he told the crow. "Stay with her and help her."

"But Merly," Ryah protested, "you told me that from the time you were a baby he has always been with you. That you've never passed a whole day without Trey."

"That's true," said Merly unhappily. He thrust Trey at Ryah. "I have to go." And turning, Merly disappeared into the forest. The crow called after him but didn't follow.

Ryah sat down and the crow hopped from her wrist to her lap. For a long time the only sound was the burble of the stream. Ryah stroked the crow absently. Finally she spoke. "I can't go before tomorrow," she said. "Meet me before dawn at the stone gateway that borders my town."

Trey blinked his eyes and nodded his beak. Then he spread his wings and flew off into the forest.

⊰ — ⊱

The next morning, Ryah slipped out of her house before the sun was up, carrying only a small loaf of bread tied in a cloth and wearing a thin cloak against the chill. "I have gone to help father," read the note she left her mother. "Don't worry. I love you and I will come back."

In the dim light, Ryah made her way through the empty streets, toward the stone portal that marked the entrance to the town. She squared her jaw as she passed by the dusty marketplace where pods were sold and dead deas returned. As she approached the large gateway, a dark shadow swooped from above and Trey landed on her shoulder. Together, the proceeded in silence on the path that climbed between the Mountain of the Sun and the Mountain of the Witch.

Ryah was strong and hiked steadily through the morning, stopping only to share some bread with Trey. The path was broad at first, because it was used for driving goats to the high summer pastures, but beyond those meadows it became narrow and faint. Without the crow, there were many places she would have lost the path, due to rock outcroppings, wild huckleberries and scrub, or game trails that crisscrossed the steepening slope. But whenever she hesitated, Trey flew ahead, calling her to a place where the path once again emerged clear and definite across a grassy clearing or in the soft dirt at a stream's edge.

By late afternoon, they reached the place where the trail split: to the left, the path led up the Mountain of the Sun; to the right, the path climbed the Mountain of the Witch. Ryah turned to the right and stared at the steep peak. It seemed impossibly far, and Ryah realized what Trey must have known from the beginning – they would not arrive that day. So as the light faded, she found a rocky hollow carved into a stream bank by the spring torrents. There, she curled herself tight, with her back pressed up against the damp, bumpy earth, and prepared herself for a long, cold, sleepless night.

Many times during the miserable hours that followed, fear overcame her determination and Ryah wished she had not come. At one point, she awoke and thought she saw a pair of yellow eyes and a moving shape across the stream. Was it her imagination? She started to drift back to sleep, but small sounds – a breaking twig and a falling pebble – would jerk her to wakefulness. Were these merely the sounds of the night? She couldn't tell.

Her only comfort was Trey, who lay warm and watchful against her chest. Once, when the blanket of darkness seemed particularly thick, he drew himself up and cawed a threat at something invisible to Ryah. After that, Ryah lay motionless, eyes straining to see, ears tuned to every whisper. Her mind began to spin deas that could be used for fighting, for fending off the monsters that she imagined in the dark. Making deas helped her feel fierce and strong, and they pushed her frightened thoughts away. As the night wore on, she surrounded herself with more and more of the faint glowing shapes.

Finally, after what seemed like an eternity, the world began to transform itself from a sea of darkness to a shadow land of gray and pink. As soon as there was enough light, Ryah set out again, stiff and shivering in her thin cloak but glad to be moving. Now, instead of focusing on deas, she occupied herself with placing her feet firmly on the steep eroded trail. Upward she climbed, the vegetation looking ever more sparse, dwarfed, and twisted by the wind. As she emerged from the last scrubby trees, the sun crept, large and red, above the misty horizon, and with its warmth, her confidence returned.

Ahead, the slopes lay covered with fallen rock and small tufts of fierce little plants eking out survival in any sheltered patch of soil. She could make out the path crossing and re-crossing the slope, before it disappeared completely over the shoulder of the mountain.

"Are we close?" Ryah asked Trey. He flapped off, following the path where it curved around the mountainside. Then he quickly returned, cawing and giving his funny nod. Sure enough, when Ryah herself had climbed the stony slope and rounded the curve, she saw in the distance the crumbling gray towers of the witch's fortress.

It was carved into the side of the mountain itself, built in an age beyond history to guard a narrow pass against enemies that only the stones now remembered. On one side, the rock wall rose sheer above it. On the other, the pass lay scooped out, windswept and stark, a place that man or beast might hurry through, hunched against the elements and driven by necessity. The fortress itself had been built with watchtowers facing either approach. The one nearest Ryah lay in ruin, broken half away, with a mound of stone around its base. From there a wall, with roof pitches showing behind it, ran straight back into the mountain face, and in it Ryah saw an entrance.

The closer she walked, the larger the fortress loomed in front of her, until she felt as small as the crow that slowly circled overhead. A massive gate stood open, askew on broken hinges. In front of it, the path passed between two standing stones, each as tall as Ryah herself. On one, ancient letters declared:

UNINVITED

And the other stone advised:

STOP HERE

Perched atop the standing stones were two black statues of regal panthers. Ryah stepped bravely between them, her eyes on the gateway. As she moved, she saw a shadow creep on the ground at her feet. Suddenly, she was knocked flat, flailing and rolling in a tangle of girl and panther, for the cats were no longer statues but real guardians of the door. Then one of the great beasts rose over her, its mouth open wide. She thought all was lost, but a small black dart fell from the sky, straight for the face of the panther! The panther released her and was off, yowling and batting at a torn ear and injured eyes.

Ryah scrambled to her feet and ran toward the gate. There she grabbed a splintered board that lay on the ground and spun to face the other panther. The first one had fled after the crow's attack, but the other panther, though also blinded in one eye, had one of Trey's wings in his mouth. Forgetting her own danger, Ryah ran toward the panther and swung the board as hard as she could. The panther opened its mouth in a hiss of pain and Trey dropped onto the ground. Now the panther turned on Ryah. But once again, Trey was in the air, swooping down on the head of the cat, clawing at its ears, pecking at its good eye, until the beast, in a fit of fury and pain, shook free of the bird and shot away across the hill.

Ryah stood gasping for breath. She wrapped her torn cloak around her injured arm and hand, where deep scratches had begun dripping blood onto the ground beside her. Trey rose high into the air, scanning the mountainside in a great circle. Then he dropped, quivering, onto her shoulder.

Ryah held out her good arm for the crow and touched his back clumsily with the bandaged hand. "You saved my life," she whispered. Then, frightened that the panthers might return as quickly as they had gone, she added, "What do we do now?" Trey touched her gently with his beak, then flew to the wall and perched himself high above the gate. With her injured arm clutched to her side Ryah ran after him, looking all the while behind her and on both sides for the dark shapes of the cats. They were nowhere to be seen.

She passed through the gate into a courtyard, where tough mountain grasses pushed up between cracks in broken pavers. The courtyard stepped upward, following the slope of the mountain. On the highest terrace, water spurted from the rock, flowing down the other levels of the courtyard in a narrow channel before it emptied into a pool, carved deep into the bedrock on which the fortress rested. On the far side of the pool, the channel continued almost level until the water disappeared beneath the fortress wall. On the wall, were large windows and a door facing the courtyard.

"Hello," Ryah called in a muted voice. She did not know whether to hide or to announce her presence. There was no response, save a red bird that perched near the pool and sang a few fluted notes. Presently, feeling bolder, Ryah walked toward the pool. The red bird gazed at her briefly and then flew inside the castle through one of the windows. *How odd*, thought Ryah. After checking once more for the panthers, she bent to wash her arm and hands.

The pool steamed and smelled faintly of sulfur. To Ryah's surprise, when she touched the water, it was warm. Curious, she stood and followed the channel until it flowed beneath the wall, and then she studied the door beside her. It seemed as weathered as the fortress itself, except that the iron hinges and latch looked well oiled and recently used. She lifted the latch, and the door swung open to her touch. Trey landed with a rustle of wings on her outstretched arm.

Inside, Ryah found herself in a damp, warm room with sunlight pouring in through high windows in the wall and ceiling. Long stone tables stretched from one end of the room to the other, save in the middle, where a fountain bubbled with the steaming water. Each table was covered with rows of clay pots in which grew exotic plants of all sorts and sizes – plants like the ones that had sprung up in the clearing attached to her father's pods.

Some of the larger plants were blooming, and in the largest of these a fruit was forming in the center of each blossom. Each fruit was a faintly colored transparent sphere which revealed, if you peered closely enough as Ryah did, an image of an object. Some of these Ryah recognized as variations on familiar gadgets or jewelry or other such items. Many were completely unfamiliar. She thought to herself, *I have found what I was looking for.*

At the far end of the room a doorway led into a room of an entirely different sort. In contrast to the first room, it seemed small and cramped. Dusty canisters and jars with strange faded labels were stacked on shelves along the walls. Lumpy cloth sacks lay scattered among them. The jars that sat open held sticks, leaves, crystals, and minerals of different kinds. On other shelves sat rows of empty jars. And at the far end of the room, a large cauldron hung above a fire that seemed to burn for fuel the air itself.

Ryah took a few steps into the room and then froze. Close to the fire, a stooped figure straightened and turned toward her. To her horror she found herself pinned in the gaze of a scarred and weathered troll – at least she thought he was a troll. He was taller than her father and wider than Merly; still he looked strangely human, though threatening and wild. *The one Merly told me about*, she thought.

The troll wore a stained leather apron with pockets that were torn or missing altogether, and he held a wooden stick with which he had been stirring the pot. Dark eyes glared out from a creased face that could have been made of the same leather as his apron. Ryah gulped and stepped backward. Instantly, the troll lurched across the room, and a gnarled hand with long broken nails shot out and grabbed her arm. "What are you doing here?" he demanded harshly.

"I – I want to see the witch," answered Ryah. She spoke boldly enough, but her knees were shaking and, in reality, she wanted nothing more than to break free and run. Trey rested on her arm, alert yet calm.

The troll opened his mouth to answer, and then let out a cackle of laughter. "See her you shall," he said, and he cackled again, showing sharp and broken teeth. He nodded past Ryah to the doorway behind her. Turning as best she could with her arm in the troll's grip, Ryah made out a tall figure in a red cloak crossing the room of tables toward them.

The witch moved between the tables unhurried, and though Ryah waited with her heart pounding in her ears, she couldn't help but notice that the witch didn't look as she expected, neither the delectable enchantress of some stories, nor the shriveled hag of others. She looked younger than old, but ageless might have been a better description. Dark hair fell thick onto her shoulders, and an intricate brooch fastened her crimson cloak about her throat. But what struck Ryah most were her eyes. They were large and green as emeralds, and they held Ryah in a gaze that would have rooted her to the ground even if the troll hadn't held her arm. Ryah had the feeling that those eyes could see through and beyond her.

The witch stopped before them, and the troll shifted to grip Ryah with his other hand so that they both stood facing her.

"Greetings, Lady Eldamaea," he said. "Look what I found sneakin' into the cannery. Says she wants to see you."

"I see," said the witch, shifting her gaze from the girl to the crow. "You may loosen her arm, Senry. She is not going anywhere." As the words were spoken, Ryah knew that she was not, in fact, going anywhere – she could not even try. "So this is the pair that brought such injury to my guardians," said the witch in a cool, stern voice. "It will challenge my herbs and skills to heal them."

"They were trying to kill us," answered Ryah, wary.

"No. They would merely have subdued you and brought you to me. Had you read the warning and waited for an escort, they would not have harmed you at all." She narrowed her eyes at Trey. "That is no ordinary bird you carry," she said.

"No," said Ryah. But she offered nothing more.

"Who are you, and why have you come here?" asked the witch. "My scouts watched you toiling for more than a day and enduring a night unfit for a human child. Only the presence of the crow kept you from being eaten in the dark. It is long indeed since a human of any age ventured into these unprotected parts."

Ryah hesitated. What should she say? But then she thought of her father, and that made her angry. She pulled herself up and the words burst out: "I am Ryah, born of Renn and Arn. I have come to make you stop taking our deas and killing them. It is wrong. They should grow and change and become what they will."

"To make me!" The witch laughed. "What power have you to make me do anything, least of all this, when the deas are freely sold and then bought by your people? It was they who approached me, not the reverse. I simply provide the means by which the deas are preserved. Would I not have been a fool to say 'no' when your people came offering me their most precious creations and their greatest power?"

"But it is wrong," insisted Ryah. "It is evil."

"You fear my power and you think me evil," said the witch, "but I am not. My kind are older than the race of humans, and my power runs as deep as the roots of this mountain. Your notions of good and evil are foreign to me. Within my realm, they are one and the same. Any 'evil' that has been done to humans through my power was done by human hands."

Then Ryah, overwhelmed and overtired, began to cry. She cried because the witch was not as she had expected and that made her feel confused. She cried because she saw that what the witch said was true, that her father's harm had come at the hands of the villagers themselves. And she cried because she now felt small and ridiculous and hopeless about her mission.

"I am foolish," she said sadly.

"No," said the witch. "Brazen, perhaps, but not foolish. The fools are your people who sit content with the hardened, shrunken deas they buy from my servant. In all these years, not one has come seeking to alter the contract that was made so long ago. The beauty of human deas and the power of their magic is as great as any power of any race that has been born onto this earth. Why do you think I entered the contract, I who can take the form of bird or beast and who have the far reaches of this mountain at my hand?"

Ryah clutched Trey against her chest and did not answer.

"Come," said the witch, "let me show you."

She led Ryah back through the room of stone tables and out into the courtyard. Up they climbed, crossing the terraces, until they reached the highest level of the fortress.

There she opened a door, and Ryah stepped into a room with the size and proportions of a chapel. It was a room of marvels. In the corners, twining vines, some as thick as her waist, climbed the walls toward a high arched ceiling. From them dangled blossoms and fruits of many colors and shapes. Tapestries covered the walls with scenes of mythical creatures and faraway worlds. Tall windows cast light that streamed golden onto furnishings unlike any Ryah had ever seen. On the tables lay trays of small objects, simple and intricate, representing animals or plants or human activities or nothing at all save the graceful curves and angles found in nature.

"I save the best for myself," said the witch, "but not hardened and preserved. These are *living* deas. They change as I attend to them." And Ryah, moving among them, could see that they did. The deas that trailed by her shoulders shone brighter and began to mingle with others that hung in the air.

The witch watched them for a while. Then she frowned when she noticed some dark deas. "These deas are curious. They are quite ugly," she said. "Why?"

"Because I made them in the night when I was scared," said Ryah. "And because of my father."

"Your father makes deas such as these?"

"No!" said Ryah. "His are beautiful and useful and wonderfully complicated … I mean they would be if he didn't have to crush them into seeds and hide them … I mean I think they would be if only … " she trailed off, because she realized she didn't know. She had never seen any of her father's deas in any form except the pods and the sprouts in the glade.

"You are here because of your father," observed the witch.

"Yes," said Ryah. Then she told about the law and how she had come home to find him gone. "If only they could see this," she said. "Then the people would know Father is right. They would see, and they would change the law."

"I find that unlikely," responded the witch. "The townsfolk had living deas before and they chose to sell them. They sell them every week without protest, except when they want to haggle for a higher price. You and your father are different, outliers, strange. The others do not want what you want."

"We can't be the only ones," Ryah protested. "There must be others too. If just for a short time, just for one month, the deas weren't made into pods. Just long enough that my people could see and remember what deas can become. If you would just let them try a different way."

"Me?" said the witch. "If *I* would just let them try a different way? They could stop selling their deas any time they choose. Why are you telling *me* to let their deas go free?"

"Because they won't stop what they are doing. They can't, because of the law and because of tradition. Some won't stop because they might get punished like my father. Some won't stop because laws are laws and they abide by them, good or bad. Some won't stop because they just do what they have always done.

"You live outside our world. You said you are outside our good and our evil. But the townsfolk feel bound to the law and cannot be released from it without your help. So I am asking you for a chance."

The witch stood silent.

"Please," said Ryah. "I am begging you."

"Oh," said the witch with a glint in her eye. "Begging now, not *telling* me? Not going to *make* me?"

"No," said Ryah, flushing. "This time I am just asking."

For a long time, the witch said nothing. At last she spoke. "The destiny of humans is determined by the will of humans. You are the first who has had the will to ask." She paused. "But why should I agree? It has taken me four generations to gather together the deas in this room, tens of years watching for the extraordinary to present itself, gleaning, culling, tending. Why should I relinquish what is, by contract, rightfully mine? What have you to offer in return?"

I have nothing to offer, thought Ryah, *I don't have anything except my torn cloak and my deas*. She opened her mouth to say as much, when abruptly she remembered that the witch had called the deas of the townspeople their "most precious creations and their greatest power." *Perhaps, just perhaps …*

"I have my deas," she said aloud, "if they could be of value to you. Maybe the deas of children are different than those you have already collected?" She felt half hopeful, half ashamed to offer something that seemed so small and transient, something that people around her had disapproved of from her earliest memory. "If Merly were here," she added apologetically, "his deas would *really* be different."

"Who is Merly?" asked the witch.

"A troll," said Ryah. "He makes the most wonderful creatures and castles from clay and rocks. He doesn't have the floating kind of deas, but we make things together in the forest, and he can make them move. He is my friend."

"Ah," said the witch, eyeing the crow. "That explains the familiar. He must be a very good friend indeed."

"Yes," said Ryah, suddenly missing him very much.

"Hmm," said the witch. "The deas of trolls and children. My courtyard is stark and dreary. If you and your friend Merly could make my courtyard come alive …"

"Oh!" said Ryah, "But Merly can't come here. If he came here, something bad would happen. If the other trolls even knew that he is my friend and that he sent Trey with me …"

"They do," said the witch.

"They do?" repeated Ryah, horrified.

"Yes," said the witch. "Trey, as you have called him, couldn't come here without them knowing. And my scouts tell me that the trolls of the lower mountain are brewing a spell, a spell they use on those who are too bold in their adventuring or in their relations with humans."

"No!" cried Ryah. "What will it do to him?"

"It is an ancient spell. In ages past, all trolls submitted themselves to it at their coming of age ceremony. They believed it preserves the character, the dark integrity of their race. But times have changed, and now it is used only to punish those who venture too far afield. When the spell takes effect, your friend will be able to leave the caves in which he lives only during the dark of night. Any ray of sunlight will turn him to stone."

"But they can't!" said Ryah. "He loves the daylight. His parents won't let them – will they?"

"His parents will submit to the will of the troll council. They may even help in preparing the potion. It is the way of the trolls."

"Is there no way to save him?" asked Ryah.

"Perhaps," said the witch. "My magic is older and stronger than the magic of the trolls. But then he would be banished from the company of trolls and the places he has spent his life. He could never return. He might not choose freedom, when the price is to lose his people and his home. Senry, who caught you in the cannery, accepted such a fate. He brings the transformed deas to your village and returns with the pods, but otherwise his is a solitary existence. I don't know that he would choose it again."

"I want to try," said Ryah.

"I see that you do," said the witch. "Find him, then. I am willing that the choice be his."

"If I can," said Ryah, "I will bring him here, and we will make the courtyard grow. Then will you grant my town a month without turning the deas to pods?"

"Yes," said the witch, bemused. "By our common Mother, you have my vow. While you are asking favors, is there anything else?"

"Well, yes," said Ryah. The witch waited. "I am hungry."

Rejuvenated by a hot lunch and provisioned by Senry with soft journey cakes and round purple fruits and boiled eggs of snow partridge, Ryah fairly fled down the mountainside. Her fear for Merly and for her father propelled her. Trey looped overhead. "Go!" she called to him. "Go to Merly. I can take care of myself." But she wasn't sure that it was true, and, anyway, Trey would not leave.

What have I done?, she thought. *Father is still in prison, and now Merly is in a kind of prison, too. Instead of one person I love being trapped, there are two.* But she pushed such thoughts aside, and focused instead on navigating her way back down the mountain, over the rugged terrain that stretched between her and home. Early on, she passed the small hollow where she had spent the night. She shivered when she thought of the witch's words.

While the daylight lasted, the power and beauty of her surroundings – the sheer rock faces and tumbled boulders across the valley, the gnarled tenacity of the highest trees, the towering solidness of those that grew lower down – made her own problems (and, in fact, all of the problems of humans and trolls) seem transient and surmountable. She felt strong and surefooted, and for a while she bounded down the trail, imagining herself a mountain goat, until the pads of her feet became tender and bruised from the rocks beneath the ever-thinner soles of her shoes.

The journey down the Mountain of the Witch was faster than the climb had been. By the last light of day, Ryah reached the high pastures outside her town where the shepherds brought their flocks in summer. She stopped and cooled her aching feet in a stream that crossed the trail. Across the meadow she could make out the gray silhouette of a stone hut, a rough summer shelter that stood empty and eerie in the early autumn dusk. It offered her no comfort now with her urgency to be home.

"I wish I had a lantern," Ryah said wistfully to Trey, who had landed on the ground beside her. She looked back at the deas that still trailed her from their night on the mountainside. "What good do you do, trailing behind me? Why don't you go in front and light the way?" She swatted at one of them and discovered, to her surprise, that it had become solid! Solid enough that when she swatted it, she knocked it aside. Solid enough that she could hold it in her hand. Was it because she had spent so long thinking about them that night, or was it because of the time in the witch's room? She reached up and grabbed at one of the other deas. It was solid too!

That gave her an idea. She found a stick that was jammed between two rocks in the stream. Then she picked some long stems that stood among the dry meadow grasses. Carefully she bound the globe-shaped deas to the end of the stick. "There," she said, satisfied. It didn't give off much light, but in the black shadow of the tall trees, it did allow her to find the sheep path. Encouraged, she set off again, this time with Trey on her shoulder.

Beneath the trees, it seemed that night had come on suddenly and completely. Only a dark gray sliver overhead showed the remains of the sunlight, and that faded fast, leaving just the dim glow of the sphere in front of her. Too tired to hurry and too anxious to linger, Ryah plodded wearily forward. It seemed the trail stretched on forever. Sometimes she imagined that she had fallen into a different world, where there existed only herself and Trey and this trail – one trail that ran from the beginning of time to its end, one trail across the whole of the wide world. She walked and walked.

Without warning, Trey dug his claws into her shoulder and made a soft churring sound in her ear. Ryah froze. She was struck by a certainty that she wasn't alone. Then she heard a rustle and breathing in the darkness beside her, and the next thing she knew, a huge hairy hand grabbed her arm. She tried to pull away, but the hand just held her tighter.

"Let go of me," cried Ryah, not even knowing who or what she was talking to. The response was a sneering laugh. In the dim light of the floating deas, Ryah made out a face that could only be a troll.

"This the one?" croaked a gravelly voice from the side of the path.

"Use your brain," responded the one who held her. "Don't you see the crow?"

"That fool, Merly!" said the first. "Keepin' company with humans! Vile, doughy, night-blind, machine-makers! We should tear this one's scrawny limbs off and roast her." Trey cawed, a harsh, angry sounding caw. "Only good human's a dead human," roared the troll. "Get out of here, crow. Go back where you belong, you traitorin' piece of dung."

Trey didn't move. He made a low clattering sound. One of the trolls growled in response and then, when Trey still didn't move, struck him off of Ryah's shoulder. She heard Trey hit dry leaves on the ground.

"No!" she sceamed.

"Come on," growled the troll to his companion. He dragged Ryah off the path and into the forest. Although they weren't on a trail, the trolls seemed to have some destination. They moved quickly through the brush, pulling Ryah behind.

The branches slapped against her, and she stumbled across roots and rocks that rose up unseen underfoot. Finally, with an impatient snort, the troll that was dragging her stopped and threw her over his shoulder. Then they moved faster through the trees, until at last the troll came to a stop and heaved Ryah onto the ground in a heap.

One of the trolls bound a rope around her ankles and then shoved her aside with his foot. He walked a few paces off and dropped with a grunt onto the ground, next to the other troll who was already squatted there. "Now what?" he grunted.

"Wait for Edher. He knows what he wants to do with this one. T'was up to me, I'd have the fire goin' already."

As they talked, Ryah wiggled into a sitting position and peered around. It seemed that she was in a small clearing with a circle of standing stones. She could make out faint stars overhead and the outline of the trolls across the clearing. The two of them continued to squat, eyeing her occasionally, and carrying on a muted conversation. After a while, one of them dug some kind of food out of his pocket and began tearing off mouthfuls, grunting and snorting while he ate.

"I don't like them things," he said, nodding at Ryah between smacking and crunching sounds. "Don't like them shiny things all hangin' 'round like that. I know humans ain't got magic, ceptin' what they borrows from witches, but them things look like magic to me."

The other one snorted. "Course humans have magic, you stinkin' oaf. Every kinda creature does, just ain't like ours. But you're a snotty hatchlin' if you're afeard of them little things."

"Go get 'em then," said the other.

"Would if I wanted to," said the first. But neither of them moved, and it dawned on Ryah that they both were afraid of the deas. Reaching up, she grabbed one of the small round spheres and flung it toward the trolls. It struck a rock in front of them and exploded into fragments of colored light that lit up the clearing and stuck to the trolls and to the rocks and everything around, for that is the kind of dea it was – made by Ryah to frighten off creatures that lurked in the darkness.

Where the pieces of deas stuck, smoke started to rise up, and the trolls began hopping and yelping, knocking the slivers of deas off of their shirts and arms and hair, as if they were sparks from a fire. By then, Ryah had another dea in each hand. She flung one of them, and it too exploded. This one burst into little blobs that began oozing down the legs and arms of the trolls, leaving streaks of glowing color.

Now the trolls danced and slapped furiously, and as Ryah raised her arm to throw a third dea, one of them roared, "Outa here!" He leaped into the trees, and Ryah could hear him crashing through the underbrush. The remaining troll lunged toward Ryah, cursing. "When I gets my hands on you …"

Bang! A dea burst in his face and a hissing cloud of purple steam rose up, blinding him so that he stumbled and tripped. He fell to the ground, rolling and thrashing. Ryah caught hold of her last trailing dea and took careful aim. It burst on the troll's leg, and stringy glowing tentacles shot out like a spider web in all directions. The troll grabbed at the webbing, but it stuck to his hand and within a moment he was caught in a hopeless tangle.

Immediately Ryah began tugging at the ropes, her fingers fumbling against the tight knots. The remains of the deas provided a little light, so she could barely see what she was doing. Then something touched her hand. She jerked it back, and a small creature hopped into her lap. Trey had found her! With his sharp beak, the crow poked and tugged, and slowly the knots loosened. Ryah quickly untied them and unwound the rope.

Meanwhile, the troll was still thrashing and roaring, but some of the sticky threads had broken. Ryah lurched to her feet and bent to scoop Trey off the ground. She clutched him against her chest with one hand and then scrambled to the other side of the tree, where she at least was out of sight of the troll. She didn't know what to do next.

"Can you see?" she murmured to Trey. "Can you guide me?" The crow gave his little churring sound that she now recognized as a "yes." Ryah thought fast. Among the trees, she couldn't see Trey at all, and she couldn't see where she was going. "Tap my hand," she said. "Tap whenever I need to change direction. One to go left, two to go right." Trey responded by tapping once.

For what seemed like hours, Ryah felt her way through the forest, guided by the gentle taps on her hand. At first she could hear the troll roaring and cursing behind her. She was terrified that he would break free and come after her or that the other troll would come, the one they had been waiting for. She wanted to make more deas like the ones she had thrown, but she couldn't stop and think about them. Moving ahead through the trees consumed all of her attention and energy.

Finally, she reached the end of the forest and could see the path to her village. It was lighter than she had expected because a late moon had risen. The moonlight pierced through the canopy of remaining trees, and their misty shadows evaporated as she emerged from the forest. "Oh, Trey," she said, "you have saved my life again." The words sounded large and loud, and, looking anxiously behind her, Ryah set off again down the trail.

It was morning before she passed through the town gates and reached the door of her house. She collapsed, exhausted, into her mother's arms. Only then, after Renn had fed hot porridge to both the girl and the bird and had turned back the bed for her daughter – "Stories can wait," her mother said – only then did Trey hop toward the door. He stopped and looked back at Ryah, and she came to him, opening the door and then kneeling to stroke his back. "Goodbye," she said. "I wish I could talk with you like Merly can. Let Merly know that I will come looking for him tonight."

But she didn't go that night, or the night after, for when she awoke in the late afternoon, she had chills and such a fever that her mother refused to let her out of the bed. "And when you do go," said Renn, "I am going with you."

Not till the third night did Ryah climb from her bed, shaky still, and insist on going to the glade. Then, after the village quieted and the moon began to rise, Renn and Ryah slipped through the streets, with Ryah bundled in her mother's warmest sweaters and squeezed into the cloak she had outgrown two winters prior.

They came to the glade unchallenged, but Merly was not there. And though they waited until the chill seeped through all those sweaters and Ryah began shivering and could not stop, even then Merly did not come. Discouraged, they returned to the house, and Ryah had a night of angry and frightening dreams. In each one, Merly was in some sort of trouble, and she tried over and over again to save him.

The next day, Ryah went with her mother to visit her father in the jail. Arn sat on a wooden bed in a dim cell lit only by a small barred window high in the wall. He looked tired and pale. He smiled at Ryah and reached out through the bars to stroke her cheek. "In three weeks there will be a trial," he said. "After that I will come home to you." His reassurance sounded hollow, though, and Ryah thought that he did not believe his own words. She shivered and touched her father's hand. She wished she could tell him about Merly and the witch and ask his advice, but the guard stood near, so she just squeezed his fingers.

"It will all work out," she whispered, trying to sound more confident than he did.

The rest of the day, Ryah helped her mother with chores. Renn had taken in extra laundry and mending from neighbors to help pay for the family's food, and mounds of clothing lay about the small house. Ryah helped by scrubbing in the courtyard, heating irons in the fireplace, and sewing by candlelight. Along with her mother, she worked into the night, until the clothes and stitching all began to blur together and she couldn't place the needle right no matter how hard she rubbed her eyes. After the moon rose, she and Renn made their way once again to the clearing, but Merly still was not there. "Merly," she called. "Trey, Trey come to me." But no one came. *How will I ever find him?*, she thought. *Maybe he has already been turned to stone.*

However, one good thing came of that trip. By the bright light of the moon, Ryah showed her mother the plants that had grown from her father's deas. Many were now as tall as she was. They crowded each other in a wild tangle of shadows. "Look," whispered Renn, "They are blooming."

Later that night, Ryah crawled into bed beside her mother. She was wondering what to do, as her thoughts started blurring into dreams. Suddenly, a sharp rap at the window startled her awake. She froze. Had she imagined it? No, there it was again. She crept to the window, pulled back the shade, and almost screamed. A strange and distorted face was mashed up against the glass, with two eyes just inches from hers. She jerked back. The other person did too and then he came into focus – there was Merly staring in at her!

"Let me in," he hissed. Ryah ran to the door and fumbled open the lock, and Merly tumbled in on top of her. "I'm sorry," he panted, picking himself up. "If humans find me in the village, they'll chase me out with stones and clubs. Trey's outside watchin'."

Renn, who had woken too, slipped out the door and shuttered the windows. Then she came back inside and lit a candle from the embers in the fireplace.

Ryah peered at Merly anxiously. She grabbed his hand and drew him to the table. "I tried to find you," she said. "The witch told me that the other trolls were going to make you drink a potion so that sunlight would turn you into stone. Did they?"

"Yes," he said bitterly. "My own parents agreed. They all said that any troll who preferred daylight to darkness and who lent his familiar to a human was 'hopelessly perverse,' and that only the potion could keep me from betrayin' my kind. *My kind!* Just 'cause I'm a troll don't mean they're my kind! I actually thought about goin' out in the daylight anyway and bein' turned to stone, just to show how little I think of their idea of what a troll should be." Then he slumped dejectedly. "Problem is – I don't wanna be turned to stone."

"There is another way," Ryah burst out. Then she slowed herself. "Actually, you might not want to do it." She told him about her encounter with the witch, all she had seen and heard, what the witch had said about the courtyard, and what she had said about reversing the spell. "By the magic of the witch you can be free to live by daylight or darkness. But then you would be banished from your family and from the company of trolls for the rest of your life. *Forever.* They would drive you away or even kill you if you tried to come back."

"I don't care," said Merly. "I hate 'em all. I'm ready to go to the witch with you tonight. Right now!"

Renn had been listening quietly in the background, warming tea for Merly and Ryah. Now she spoke. "I don't know you, Merly, but a decision such as this is enormous. It is bigger than whatever hurt and anger you may be feeling. As humans grow older, community and family become more and more important. It must be the same for trolls. If you can, try to put aside the feelings of the moment and also your desire to help Ryah, because you have other matters to weigh. You need to think *both* about the life you would be embracing and the one you would be leaving. Think about all you would gain, but think also of all you would lose. When you can feel both possibilities, as real and large as they are, then you will be ready to choose."

Merly scowled, but Ryah reached out and touched his hand. "My mother is right," she said. "You know what you want to do right now, but you need to think about the rest of your life. At first it will be wonderful. Think of our deas coming alive in the courtyard! But what about afterward? You are my friend forever, but I can't live with you in the forest, and it will never be safe for you here in my village."

Merly was silent for a long time. Renn set the tea down in front of him and he picked it up absently, staring at the shiny curve of the cup without seeing it. Ryah and Renn waited. At last he shook his head as if to clear it. "I think I know what I want," he said, "but I'll wait till tomorrow to decide fer sure. Can you meet me at the glade after dark?"

"Yes," Ryah answered, with a glance at her mother.

"Yes," confirmed Renn. "We will come prepared for you to leave or to stay." With that, Merly set down the cup, and with an awkward little bow to Renn and a hug for Ryah, he took his leave.

The next night at the glade the words burst out of his mouth as soon as he saw them. "I may be sorry, but I still wanna go. I don't know how my life'll be or where I'll live, but I can't imagine spendin' year after year like this. I'd rather take the chance!"

He seemed so poised to defend his decision that Ryah laughed. "We aren't going to stop you, Merly, just let us catch our breath. Mother said we would be ready either way, and we are. We've brought food and water for the journey."

Renn held out a flask and a small bundle tied with rope so that it could be worn as a pack. "I confess I'm afraid," she said. "I'm afraid for the two of you traveling in the dark – who knows what you may encounter? And it will be difficult to find a place for Merly to sleep during the day out of the sunlight. I'm also afraid the witch may change her mind and find some other use for you. I know you trusted her, Ryah, but what if it was all deception and lies? What if you misread her?"

"I didn't!" Ryah scowled. "We've talked about this more than once. Besides, I already told you …"

"I can see as well in dark as I see in daylight," Merly broke in. "Below the summer pastures, the only danger fer me are trolls, and them I know how to avoid, believe you me. Beyond that, well, if Ryah made it with Trey, fer sure we can all make it together. I'm stronger than I look and faster too."

"I imagine so," said Renn. "It's just that there are so many unknowns. And with Ryah's father in jail," her voice got shaky, "I can't come with you or come after you if something goes wrong."

At the quiver, Ryah's irritation melted and she put an arm around her mother. "It will be all right," she said. "I promise."

"Never promise what you cannot know," murmured Renn. Nevertheless, she pulled her daughter close. Then, abruptly, she stepped back. "Go," she choked, giving Ryah a small push with her hands. "Go – only because I see no other way. If you have not returned after your father's trial, we will come after you. Or I will, if …"

"I'll take care of her," Merly said.

"We'll take care of each other," Ryah added. But Renn had already turned away. She disappeared into the darkness, and they could hear her on the stones and among the branches, fumbling her way back toward town.

The two friends stood in silence for a moment, listening. "Come on," said Merly. "Let's get movin'. We can cut 'round the village. If we stay close to it, our noise won't matter so much, and other trolls don't come 'round here."

"Good thing," said Ryah, "because I can barely see my own hands tonight. I could walk into a tree as easily as walking around one. I'll have to follow you."

They set off through the forest. Ryah stumbled and lurched along behind Merly, struggling to keep up. Once they reached the trail, his pace grew even faster, relentless. After the second time she tripped, sprawling, Ryah snapped, frustrated to tears. "Merly, I can't do this. You know I can't see the ground."

He stopped then and paused for Ryah to get upright. "I'm sorry," he said, edgy but apologetic. "I didn't want to say this in front of your mother, but I don't think there'll be any place safe fer me when the sun comes up. I gotta get there tonight … or not at all."

Ryah stared at him in stunned silence. *Of course … those bare slopes … his impatience.* Now, finally, she put the pieces together. "I'm holding you back," she exclaimed in dismay. "You need to go on without me."

"I should have, but it's too late. I didn't think … I thought … I don't know *what* I thought. But we've come too far now. You can't go back alone, and I can't take you back."

"Can we go another night? We could go back home and …"

"No. You don't understand. I can't! My parents know I've been actin' strange. They asked me all sorts of questions 'bout last night. They may be lookin' fer me right now, close to town. If the other trolls find out what I am tryin' to do, do you know what my punishment will be?"

"No."

"They'll put me out in a clearin'. Tie me up. And wait fer the sun to rise."

"No! Then I definitely am going back home alone and you are going on! It took me more than a day to get to the fortress last time. Together we don't stand a chance!"

"And if the trolls find you, then what? You think they won't figure out where I am? You think they won't come after me?"

"Can Trey warn me? Can he go ahead or something? Where is he, anyway?"

"I don't know where he is. I thought he'd stay close to us, but he flew off right after we left the glade."

Ryah slumped, defeated. "I'm going to kill you!" she wailed.

"I can carry you," said Merly. "Trolls are stronger than humans. We can leave the clay."

"No," said Ryah. "No, don't carry me. I'll do better. I can run. You go as fast as you would without me, and I'll keep up." And she did for a long while, jogging behind him with the awkward, exhausting gait of someone who doesn't know exactly where her feet are going to fall. She kept up until she could go no further, not even at a walk, not even at a crawl, and then Merly hauled her onto his back, like he had said, and kept going.

Somewhere above the tree line, somewhere in the fields of tumbled boulders and loose gravel, Ryah jerked herself out of the dull stupor that had settled over her as she clung to Merly's lurching shoulders. The darkness was changing, a barely perceptible shift from the black of emptiness to the black of coal. The difference was subtle but definite. "Merly!" she called out, "Merly, put me down. Dawn is coming!" But he plodded forward as if he hadn't heard. She wriggled. Finally, Merly dropped her heavily on her swollen feet, so that she staggered and nearly fell.

"I know," he said in a flat voice. It was the voice of one without hope. It was her father's voice, and it terrified her.

"You can't give up!" Ryah cried. She grabbed his arms and peered into his face, pleading. "Please, Merly. You've got to go on without me now. It's your only chance. Run if you can, please, before it is too late. It isn't that far."

Merly blinked at her, unmoving at first, but she must have called up some glimmer of hope, for he suddenly straightened and drew a big gulp of air. "Go," said Ryah, seizing the moment, "Go!" And like Renn did in the glade, she gave him a small push. Merly turned, and ran up the faint trail into the last dregs of the night. The hillside was steep and the path folded back on itself, and for a short while Ryah could hear him gasping above her. Then she was alone.

She stood for a time, staring at the place where he had disappeared. Then slowly, she limped after him, carefully placing one foot in front of the other on the rough stones that were emerging from the darkness. Even as she strained to see them, she wished desperately that she could not. Never had she so longed for the darkness to last, never had she watched so intently as her charcoal surroundings took on form and depth and faded into layers of gray. "Please," she begged the sun, "Please wait." But the sun does not wait for man or beast, life or death, and long before she had reached the final rise, pink threads began appearing in the eastern sky.

He has already made it, she told herself in the final minutes before the sunrise. *I will find him in the room of plants or by the fire, warm, with Senry and a cup of hot tea, or in the great room with the witch …*

Then she rounded a curve and her heart gave a terrible lurch. Her dreams fell away like broken glass. There he was, sitting on a rock ahead of her with his head bowed, facing the Mountain of the Sun.

Ryah's throat clamped aching shut and she stumbled to him and dropped onto her knees. Unable to find words, she laid her head in his lap and wrapped an arm around one of his thick legs. Merly put a hand on her head. "My ankle," he said, oddly apologetic. "I stepped wrong on it and it won't work." Then he lifted his face toward the mountain and waited.

Ryah couldn't bear to watch. She closed her eyes tight. *Any minute*, she thought, *any second, I will feel Merly turn to stone.* But what came to her next wasn't the feeling of a warm body turning to cold stone. It was a sound – a whirring sound and vibration. She opened her eyes and for an instant thought that night had returned, that someone, somehow had turned back the clock. The sky to the east was black again, so black she could no longer see the outline of the mountain. Then she realized that the black was a cloud, moving rapidly toward them. Then the cloud turned into birds … crows … a great flock of black crows … as far as she could see!

"Trey!" Ryah breathed in wonder. She sat up and stared. Now the flock was directly overhead. The birds began circling like a giant black whirlpool, dipping into the valley to the east so that not a single ray of sunlight could break through. Out of the vast cloud of crows, a single black spot broke away and moved toward them. Trey fluttered to the ground in front of Merly and Ryah. He opened his mouth in a loud caw, then took to the air again and disappeared into the flow of circling birds.

Merly sat as still as if he had been turned to stone. Then suddenly he gave a great shout and began to laugh. "I'm alive!" he shouted.

He jumped to his feet – then sat back down very quickly. In his thrill at discovering himself yet among the living, he had forgotten about his ankle.

Ryah scrambled to her feet. "Lean on me," she said.

"Right," said Merly, looking highly doubtful.

Ryah hunched herself to look like a troll and spoke in the deepest voice she could muster. "I'm stronger than I look and faster too. And I can see as well in dark – *darkness of crows anyway* – as I see in daylight." Merly laughed and got up again, more gingerly this time, and they set off up the path, hobbling and shuffling and looking for all the world like some strange and decrepit animal, but filled with the new energy of hope.

The surge of relief carried them over the first few rises and folds of the trail, but as it wore off, a weary strain settled back onto both of them. The going was slow, and they had no idea how long the crows could keep flying. Their progress got slower and slower until it seemed they were scarcely making progress at all. And they were both in pain.

Fully exhausted, Merly tripped and came down heavily on his injured ankle. When he could speak between clenched teeth, he said, "I have to stop, Ryah. I have to rest, even if it's just fer a few minutes."

Ryah didn't answer. She knew he could go no further. She helped him lower himself onto a boulder beside the path and opened the skin which held their last few sips of water. "Here," she said. "I'm not thirsty."

What will we do?, she wondered. She noticed, for the first time, a small line of crows leaving the swirling flock. Merly saw it too. "They're going, aren't they," he said. He sagged, fear returning to his face.

"No," said Ryah. "Look." She pointed to another line of crows returning to the mass. "They are only resting, probably at the stream."

It gave her some hope, the thought that the crows were resting. They were not on the verge of falling, as she had feared, in a rain of feathers from the sky, or disappearing en masse over the horizon, or dispersing to their homes like a cloud of vanishing smoke. She sat down herself and watched them, mesmerized by the flowing stream and by the occasional single crow that darted across the black current to disappear again among his fellows.

"Ryah," Merly interrupted in a low, urgent voice.

She looked down at him and then followed his eyes across the slope. Moving quickly toward them over the hillside were two black streaks, two shadows within the shadow that contained them all. Ryah recognized the panthers of the witch.

Merly had drawn a knife from his belt. Ryah glanced down at it and back at the cats. "Wait," she said under her breath. "Don't make us enemies if we are not. It's possible they bear a message." All the same, she could feel her heart pounding as the panthers bounded effortlessly across a field of boulders and landed on muffled paws in front of them.

Strong and sleek they stood, with grave eyes and impenetrable faces, surprisingly unscarred by Trey's attack at the gates of the fortress. The witch's healing arts had worked well. If anything, the cats seemed even larger than Ryah remembered them, but they made no threatening move. They merely stood in silent dignity, watching.

Ryah bowed, as gracefully as she could. "Welcome, guardians of the castle of the witch. Please know that we tread these lands now at her invitation." She spoke carefully, searching for proper words, noble words from the old stories her mother had shared. She continued,

"I beg your pardon for the injury inflicted on you at our prior meeting. My companion and I thought our lives in danger. We did not fight out of ill intent, but only to save ourselves."

One of the cats bowed his head slightly. The other stepped forward and dropped at Ryah's feet a small ball of crumpled paper. She unfolded it and read:

I have asked of the guardians that they bear you to safety.
Know that I do not ask this of them lightly.
Nor lightly do they grant such a request.

On the backs of the panthers, Merly and Ryah fairly flew to the fortress, as the stony slope fell away behind them. Ryah had thought it would be difficult to balance, but the cats moved with such elegance and precision that she found herself moving in synchrony with the rhythm of the long strides. Above them the crows circled, still centered on Merly. Soon the standing stone pedestals rose up before them, and then the castle gate. In the courtyard, the panthers slowed, padding silently across the cobblestones. The door of the growing room swung open, and Senry stepped out.

He led them through another door and down a flight of stairs that seemed to descend into the mountain itself. Deep below the fortress, they came into a hall lit by small flames that hung suspended along the walls above their heads. Again, Senry opened a door. He gestured them into a room that was clearly meant for the two of them. Cots stood against two walls. A small round table held a basket of fruit and a platter of breads and cheese. A pitcher stood beside two glasses and a smaller vessel. Senry pointed to the small container and said, "You'll find somethin' in there to ease your pain, young troll. I'll tend your ankle and take you to the witch after you've rested." Then he left.

Ryah and Merly woke, disoriented, to a rapping at the door. In that deep room, no change in light or sound or air gave any indication of the hour or the passage of time. The rap repeated itself and Senry entered. He brought robes and thick towels, and he led them through the winding hall and up the stairs, back past the steaming pool in the courtyard. Stars glittered overhead in the night sky.

Below the pool, the water was no longer diverted to the growing room but flowed through deep narrow channels into two small rooms that served as bathhouses. Ryah stepped shivering from the brisk night air into one of the rooms. She stepped into the warm water and thought she had never felt anything so delicious in her life.

At length she heard a yelp from the other bathhouse and guessed (correctly) that Merly's ankle had been set. He emerged, still unable to put weight on it, but with the break straight and bound. "It hurts less already," he marveled. "I wonder what's in the gunk he used to coat my ankle before bindin' it."

"Hurry, now," said Senry, after they had eaten again. "The witch wants to see you before sunrise." They found her in the growing room, waiting.

"These three," she said to Senry, pointing to three of the plants. "Take them to the great room when they are ready." Then she turned to Merly. He bowed awkwardly. "You are welcome, young troll, young seeker."

"I thank you, kind witch, most sincerely fer rescuin' me," said Merly, fumbling for formal words as Ryah had done with the panthers.

"You are welcome," said the witch.

Merly continued in his best tongue, "Ryah says you have the power to free me from a curse cast on me by my kinsmen – a bad awful curse."

"Truly, the worst curses are cast by kin," said the witch wryly. "Some are curses of indifference, others of misguided kindness, and still others of ill intent. Humans deny that this is so, preferring to see their enemy in the stranger, the other, the alien-born. But trolls, by necessity, see more clearly the dual nature of such relationships.

"It also is true that I can free you so that you are not bound to the night. But once done, I cannot gain you readmission to the community of your kind. The stone curse is a long-standing tradition of your people. It guards a way of life that they have preserved from a time before the age of men. It binds you to them, and if I break it, you will be cast adrift. Thereafter, you will have no safe passage to the land of your childhood."

"What about Senry?" asked Merly. "He walks the paths that I call home."

"He may walk them, but he dare not linger. He passes unharmed only because that region has never been home *to him*. Rather, the caves where he was born lie to the west of these peaks. Even so, if he spoke with your people or sought hospitality, they would judge him an outcast and would, by honor's code, kill him too."

Merly gulped. "May I ask one more question, my Lady? If Senry doesn't tell anybody he was freed from the curse, how'd they know?"

"Look at him," said the witch. "What do you see?" She beckoned to Senry, who had stepped away from the conversation and was marking the three plants the witch had identified for her collection. Senry came and stood beside her.

Merly looked at him closely. "Human eyes," said Merly. "And human stance. He holds himself too straight-up for a troll. And his hands – they're bigger than human hands, but the shape's all wrong fer a troll – his fingers are too long." He hesitated. "So what's he look like without his disguise, without the shape-changin' spell you cast that makes him look human so he can work in the village?"

Senry let out a loud cackle. "You think this a disguise, young Merly?" He laughed again, a softer laugh, though. Sympathetic, it seemed.

"What you see is Senry himself," said the witch. "The only disguise he wears is a troll mask that covers his face when he passes through the forest between here and the village. And that disguise cannot be worn for long.

"Senry did change shape when he drank the potion that reverses the curse. So will you, if you make the same choice. But I don't determine the shape. Only trolls, accursed trolls, can be turned to stone by daylight. And only by relinquishing the brotherhood of trolls can you be free of the curse."

"I don't understand what you're sayin'," said Merly.

"The potion Senry drank changed him from a troll to what he had, in fact, become by virtue of his decision to break with his kind. In other words, his body took the form that his defiant spirit had already taken. When he declared his independence and decided to drink the potion, he was changed forever, both inside and out."

Merly stared from the witch to Senry as her words sank in. "D-do you mean that if I drink the potion to get rid of the curse, I – I – I'll look like Senry?" he stammered.

"No," said the witch. "You will look like you – whoever *you are* inside."

It was days before Merly could bring himself to make a choice. Meanwhile, he and Ryah dove into their promised labor. The witch, either by magic or by more ordinary means, procured the bundle of clay that Merly and Ryah had abandoned along the trail, and more besides. It sat in mounds on the floor of their room beneath the fortress, where the table was rapidly taken over by a myriad of creatures, great and small. Ryah worked urgently under the pressure of her father's impending trial. *If only the witch could make the law change before then*, she thought. And Merly worked urgently with a desperate need to avoid the decision in front of him.

Ryah made stars with twining tendrils, crows with exotic tails that trailed behind them, winged hares with fish scales, and owl-eyed mice with jumping legs and marsupial pockets. She also made plants with leaves that were spiked and crenellated, furled and twisted, and with stems that were thick or feathery, wide or long, and some bearing blossoms as alien as the far reaches of her imagination.

Merly made miniature trolls with fins and gills, trolls that had wings and tails like monkeys, and trolls with wide flapping ears that could bear them aloft. He also made trolls with eyes like cave fish, and feline trolls with whiskers and tails, and trolls with two sets of arms and fur covered feet.

One morning, Merly started shaping a troll with two heads when suddenly Ryah shouted, "Stop!"

"Why?" said Merly, startled.

"The witch said that if you drink the potion, you would look like you! Like who you are on the inside," Ryah stated firmly. "So you're not going to turn into some strange beast that you don't recognize."

Merly thought about her words. He thought about them through the next two trolls, one with a lion's mane and body, the other with thin suction-cup fingers like a tree frog. "I will if I go back," he said at last.

That night they went to see the witch. "I'm ready," Merly told her. He met her eye, and his voice was strong and resolute. "It may be a long time before I find a new home, but I'll be searchin' by daylight."

"Very well," said the witch.

In the cold hour before the dawn, Merly and Ryah were awakened once more by Senry. In the courtyard blazed a fire that lit every stone and cast black shadows around the corners and below each stair. Frost glittered high on the walls, but near the fire the paving stones were dry and hot. Around the base of the fire, a black ring had been marked on the stones. The witch stood just outside the ring facing the fire, chanting words that flowed like molten silver. In her hand she held a chalice, engraved with a line of runes and symbols that wrapped around it in a spiral from the base to the rim.

Presently, she stopped chanting and passed her hand three times over the cup. Then she turned to Merly. "It is time," she said. Her eyes burned like the flames beside her. "Drink of the chalice, till you see reflected in its emptiness the face that you have worn these mortal years. Only then may you pass into the heart of the cleansing fire. It will burn away all that is immaterial to your spirit, leaving your essential and eternal form."

Ryah squeezed Merly's hand then released it. He bravely stepped forward to accept the cup from the witch. She passed it to him and said, "With this drink, you may return again to the land of the living. We await you here."

Merly took the goblet in both hands and peered into its depths. He lifted the chalice to his lips and drained it in a few large gulps. Other than a small cough, nothing happened. He handed the cup back to the witch.

"Walk boldly," she said. "Fear burns harsher than any flame."

"Go ahead," said Senry. "It doesn't hurt once you're in it."

Ryah saw Merly put one foot inside the ring and jerk it back. He hesitated, then he clenched his fists and leaped into the fire … and disappeared.

Seconds passed, then minutes. Ryah waited, hovering at the edge of the ring until it felt like the back of her was frozen and her face and arms were flushed and burning. She rubbed her hands together and tried to fight back a wave of panic that surged rhythmically with the beat of her heart. *What if the witch had erred?* she thought. *What if the potion had been mixed too small or some minor ingredient was wrong?*

And then, there he was: Merly himself, as sturdy and solid as ever. He stood among the flames but then the fire disappeared. Now, the ring held only Merly, who blinked at them with an expression of awe and wonder on his face.

As the witch had promised, he looked like himself. In fact, Ryah thought he looked more himself than ever, as if before she had seen him through a dirty pane of glass or as if he had been sketched or sculpted by a beginning artist who could not yet express his vision.

It was hard even to say what exactly had changed. She thought his face looked older somehow, but then he moved slightly and it seemed younger than before. Wiser, she thought. No, more mischievous.

Merly looked down at his hands and flexed his fingers and laughed. They were the hands of an artisan, not delicate looking nor rough, but long-fingered and well used.

"Do you recognize me?" he asked Ryah.

"Of course," she answered. "You don't look very different to me at all."

"Actually, he looks quite different," said the witch, laughing. "It is just that you, Ryah, have long seen through to his essence. That is the nature of true friendship."

"Congratulations," said Senry. He put a large hand on Merly's shoulder. "You now belong nowhere – and everywhere."

"For now, he belongs here," said the witch, "for as long as it suits him." She turned to Merly. "There is work here among the deas if you desire it."

Merly's face lit up. "Thank you, my Lady," he cried. "I have dreamed of it, but I didn't dare to ask."

The witch nodded. "You may call me Eldamaea, as Senry does." Then she turned with a swirl of her cloak and strode up the steps and out of sight.

When she was gone, Ryah gave a squeal and threw her arms around Merly. "Oh, Merly, it is better than you ever hoped!"

Senry stood by them with a smile on his face, the first they had seen. "Would you like to watch the sunrise?" he asked. He led them across the courtyard to a sheer outcropping below the fortress wall, and Merly greeted the sun with outstretched arms.

All that day – in the sunlight – Ryah and Merly carried their creations from their dim sleeping chamber to the courtyard. Unaccustomed to the light and the chill air, they squinted and shivered, but Merly sang as he worked and fairly danced up and down the stairs.

Gradually, the lowest level of the courtyard was transformed. Ryah's vines crept up the sides of the steps. Merly's trolls clustered at the edge of the pool. The flat expanses of paving stone became inhabited by families of creatures that engaged each other, or hid ineffectively among the sparse grasses, or stood as if boldly exploring their new homes. Little faces peered out of cracks in the stone walls and around the corners of the bathhouses.

One afternoon as they paused to admire their work, Senry emerged from the growing room. "Ah," he growled, squatting to examine the cluster by the pool. "What's this place becomin'?" But he sounded pleased.

"Animate them," Ryah whispered to Merly. He moved his hands and the miniature trolls started swaying and stepping. One hopped toward Senry, who was so startled that he lost his balance and toppled backwards. Merly snorted and Ryah clamped her hand over her mouth, watching to see if Senry was angry. But he merely picked himself up and continued to peer at the creatures.

Then Senry frowned. "Hmm … I once had a similar skill." He scratched the side of his cheek with one finger and squinted as if peering deep into his memories.

Suddenly one of the creatures turned and bounded across the paving stones, landing in Merly's lap. Merly jumped to his feet with a yelp and stumbled back a step, tripping over the stair on which he had been sitting, and landing on top of Ryah beside him. The clay creature tumbled to the ground and then righted itself, and in three springing leaps, it rejoined the cluster by the edge of the pool.

As Ryah and Merly untangled themselves, a loud rattling sound rose up by the pool, and Ryah realized that Senry was laughing. Then she and Merly began laughing too. They laughed until Senry picked himself up and went shuffling off to complete his chores. Then they pulled themselves together to begin again with their work.

"This is a good place," said Ryah.

"Maybe not fer all," said Merly, "but it's good fer me."

"For many," said Ryah. "I wish my father were here." In a flash her happiness vanished. She turned and fled down the stairs.

Merly caught up with her in the hallway. "Tomorrow is the trial, isn't it?"

Ryah nodded, not trusting her voice.

"Listen, we've almost finished the first level. It's sparse, but I don't think the witch expects us to fill it all at one go. Why don't you ask her if she'll do somethin' now? Maybe, when she sees all the work we've done, she won't mind if we finish the other levels after."

"But that is not what I committed," choked Ryah, "and it is not what she agreed. Anyhow, what difference would it make now, if Senry stopped going to the village?"

"Then I'll ask," said Merly. When Senry returned, Merly asked if they might speak with the witch.

"If you can find her," Senry answered, "then it means she's willin' to be found. I suggest lookin' in the great room." Merly took Ryah firmly by the hand and together they went to seek the witch.

The door of the great room swung open to their knock, and they found Eldamaea seated below a window at a carved table stacked with heavy books. While they waited, she traced her finger across the last few lines of a page, then looked up. Merly explained their request.

"You are finished with your work?"

"No," he answered honestly.

"You are finished with the lowest terrace?"

"Well, no. But we'll carry on the same whether you help Ryah now or not. And fer her, time matters. If things start changin' in the town, the people there are less likely to think Ryah's father is a criminal. But if he's convicted – I don't know exactly how these human trials work – it may be harder to get him set free."

Eldamaea turned to Ryah. "What have *you* to say?" she asked sternly.

"I am ashamed to ask for more," said Ryah, "because I have nothing more to offer. Only what I am doing already."

The witch's face softened. "I have seen what you are doing, and it is good. You may sleep easily this evening. Your wish is granted."

"It is granted?" Ryah echoed. She wasn't quite sure that she had heard right.

"Yes," said the witch. "It is already granted. Senry hasn't delivered any powder since you were last here. I have known that you would follow through. The townsfolk ran out of the powder several days ago and they can no longer turn deas into pods."

For the second time in their brief acquaintance, Ryah ran out of words and burst into tears in the presence of the witch. Merly put an arm around her. "Thank you," he said, looking up. "You've done much fer us both, more than we can ever repay."

"She appeals to me," the witch responded. "She asks for herself and for others without differentiating, without diminishing one or the other. And your friendship appeals to me, the irrationality of it, the simplicity."

She nodded at Trey, who had followed them through the door and now rested on a coat tree carved to look like a polished but wind-gnarled tree. He had taken to spending time there with Eldamaea, usually entering the room through a small open window, and the witch allowed it. "Crows are better at perceiving character than either humans or trolls, and Trey perceives value beyond life in both of you. I agree with the crow."

Merly nodded politely, as if he would need to consider her words later. "Thank you," he repeated.

The witch inclined her head and resumed reading. The audience had ended.

Five days later, while Ryah and Merly were arranging whimsical creatures and structures on the second terrace, the panthers padded through the gate followed by a pair of scruffy travelers. One carried a large cloth sack on his back, like a peddler who could not afford a mule. Ryah eyed them with curiosity and then let out a loud shriek. "Mother! Father!"

She darted across the courtyard, dodging the creations that were already in place, leaping over the water channels and up the stairs, and threw herself into her mother's arms. Her father barely had time to swing the sack off of his back before he was caught in the same embrace.

Merly, who had followed Ryah, stood to the side, playing with the sleeve of his shirt. Ryah grabbed hold of his arm and drew him in to the reunion. "He wouldn't leave me, even though I slowed him down. He put his life in danger."

"Such a gift is rare indeed," said Arn, shaking Merly's hand. "I hope that one day I may come to earn your friendship as my daughter has."

Merly flushed with pleasure.

Renn laid her hand on his arm. "I am glad to see you again," she said. "You look different by daylight, Merly."

"I guess you couldn't see him clearly before," said Ryah, with a wink at Merly.

Ryah took her parents to the growing room to meet Senry and Eldamaea. "Wait here," Senry said. "I'll see if the witch is willin' to meet with you." While they waited, Arn set his bag gently by the door and walked the aisles between the plants, examining the flowers and budding fruit.

Ryah pointed out the plants that had been marked. "These are the ones the witch will keep for herself," she said.

"I can see why," said Arn. "I can see why."

"Come!" called Senry. "A meal is set fer you. Eldamaea will join you after you eat." Arn bent to pick up his bag. "You can leave your things here," Senry said. "They're safe."

"I have a gift for your mistress," said Arn. "Should I leave it in your care?" He opened the bag, revealing a mound of translucent red fruit like those growing around them. "Fruit from the glade," he said. "Produced by the choicest of my deas that were cast away. From what I have heard, this is the one thing I have that Eldamaea might value. And she is the one with whom I wish to share the first of my deas set free."

Senry bent to examine the soft round fruit. He picked one up and turned it over in his hand, then another. "These ones are different than any I've seen," he said, his eyes gleaming with pleasure. "Yes, leave 'em with me. I'll advise Eldamaea of your gift."

They ate by the hearth in a simple warm kitchen, at a round table with no two chairs alike, yet each as sturdy and right as if all other kitchen chairs were somehow lesser descendants. A wooden birdcage hung by the window, and a red bird sang to the sunlight. Ryah recognized it as the bird she saw by the pool when she first came to the castle. "The cage door is open," she said to Senry.

He glanced up. "So it is," he said. "That bird comes and goes as she pleases."

As Senry set a large bowl of steaming soup before Arn, he observed dryly, "There are, among humans, many who'd not eat the fare of a witch served by a troll."

Arn nodded. "True indeed. And there are those among us who would not eat a meal prepared by a mayor and served by a magistrate – those who have learned that, in a world where things are not always what they seem, it may be safer to dine with witches and trolls than with bureaucrats." Senry smiled and nodded and pulled up a chair to join them at the table, and Ryah thought that men had a most peculiar code for revealing themselves to each other.

"I'm curious," said Senry. "What's happened in town since I stopped bringin' the powder? How came it to be that you are here a free man?"

"The first part you will have to ask Renn," answered Arn. "All that I can tell you by my own experience is this: On the day scheduled for my trial, I was awakened early by a guard. He brought me to the prison courtyard and demanded that I bathe at the well, which I was only too glad to do. While I washed he glared at me. 'I wonder if this trouble is all *your* fault,' he said, but I didn't know what he meant. Then he led me to the courtroom.

"There I encountered a remarkable scene. Several in the room, including the judge and the prosecutor, were trailed by floating deas like those that follow Ryah much of the time. They seemed most embarrassed. I saw the prosecutor try to brush his deas aside before beginning his arguments, but his hand just went right through them. Someone laughed. Then he launched into a long dull statement about the nature of my crime, but I think that one of his deas must have caught the attention of the judge, for suddenly it skipped across the small distance between them and joined the two deas that hovered by the judge's shoulder. That drew a lot more laughter.

"They appeared as fools, sitting in judgment over me and arguing that I should be punished for keeping unsold deas, when their own deas were visible to all. In the end, the judge, a man of fair integrity I think, as much as said so. I was released with a stern warning and a threat of dire consequences should I ever again be caught with unlicensed deas … but even that admonishment sounded ridiculous given the context. 'And what's he supposed to do with them?' someone shouted from the back of the courtroom. The judge just pounded his gavel and dismissed my case. Afterward, there were plenty of townspeople who congratulated me.

"After we left the courtroom, Renn told me how Ryah discarded my dea pods in the glade, about her friend Merly, and about her seeking help from the witch. We packed up and went straight away to the glade, collected the dea plants, and then set out to find our daughter."

Renn laughed. "The first time you failed to appear at the market, Senry, people speculated that you were simply ill. Those who make deas to sell continued apace, and the traders continued to buy them up, confident that you would return at the next market. But the following week, when you were absent again, things began to get interesting. People started running out of pod powder and soon deas were floating everywhere.

"Then the mayor issued an emergency order requiring that all remaining powder be turned over to the authorities. But what they collected wasn't enough to go around, so the deas multiplied! We heard rumors that the mayor sent a party to make inquiries of the witch, but for some reason they could not find the trail up the mountain. I have to say, I don't understand, since we found the trail easily enough."

Senry chuckled at this, and Ryah remembered what he said to her about finding the witch: *If you can, it means she is willing.* "Go on," Senry said to Renn.

"Out of necessity, the law was suspended. Many creative minds were in the habit of generating deas for sale and they couldn't stop. More and more deas began appearing – in the streets, in the schools, at the marketplace. While the authorities tried frantically to corral the deas, first young people and then older ones, too, started playing with the deas, bumping them into each other, shaping them according to curiosity and whim. Some disapproved and lobbied the mayor to restore order, but it was too late. As we left town, deas were literally everywhere – who knows where it will end?"

"We'll see," said Senry with a smile.

They continued to speculate about the "deas revolution," as Arn called it, until finally the eating and conversation slowed. Then Arn asked, "Do you think Lady Eldamaea is ready for us now?"

Senry looked up before answering, "Yes. I believe she is." Ryah followed his gaze to the birdcage and noticed that the red bird was flying out the window.

Senry escorted them all to the great room, and then he turned to Merly and said, "Come help me take care of those fruits," and the two trolls departed.

So Ryah was left to introduce her parents to Eldamaea, who sat waiting at the end of the room in her velvet red cloak. "My parents," she said to the witch, "Renn and Arn." She spoke with a voice that was both shaky and fierce, like when she had first stood before the witch.

Arn felt the full weight of the room, with its magnificent furnishings, artwork, and tapestries. He felt the presence of a wise one before him as well. He looked humbly at the witch and said, "I have sought audience with you, but I doubt there is anything I can say that you do not already know, or anything I can offer that does not already lie within your power."

"Much that is known is worth repeating," said the witch, "and your gift of fruit pleases me very much."

"With your permission, I would stay with my daughter and assist her," said Arn. "When she has completed her work, I will escort her home."

"You may stay with Ryah," said Eldamaea. Then she turned her soulful green gaze upon Renn.

"Also with your permission, I would stay with my daughter and tend her," said Renn, "and all else here that is within the realm of my tending."

"That would be Merly," said the witch. "He is still young and in need of a mother's love. Senry, too, needs some tending. He built a wall around his heart these many years and he now constructs a gate. I suspect you will help open it."

"I understand," said Renn.

As the family walked back across the great room and out into the courtyard, Ryah's heart leapt with pride. It seemed to her that her parents were just as important and impressive as anything in the castle, including its grand furnishings, fine art, dancing deas … and even its mysterious matron.

☙ —— ❧

Their labor lasted for weeks. Father and daughter and troll worked tirelessly filling the witch's courtyard with spirit filled creations. At one point, though, Arn became concerned regarding the length of their stay.

"It will be all right," said Renn. "The house is shuttered against storms, and I gave the chickens to old Enya, who lost hers to a wolf."

Yet, the hardest part was not knowing what was happening in town. Would deas or pods be banned when they returned? Would the deas be bright or dark? Otherwise, the weeks were a total pleasure. In spite of the austerity of their rooms and the deepening cold of coming winter, each guest was occupied pursuing his own skill, her own pleasure.

At last, the highest terrace of the courtyard was completed. A peculiar tangle of life, sculpted in clay, lay seeded in the corners and around the water channels. Together, the artists went to see the witch. "Will it last the winter?" they asked. "Will the clay resist the weight of the snow and the battering of spring rains?"

"I will take care of that," said Eldamaea. "That is my domain. It will last till your grandchildren have grandchildren, though you might not recognize it. Tomorrow morning you will see."

But the next morning they did not see, for the first heavy snow had fallen, and the courtyard lay buried in white drifts. Ryah and Merly were crushed. They stood side by side and stared gloomily at the blanket of white, Ryah in an oversized wool coat that her mother had carried up the mountain, and Merly in his rolled up sleeves and bare feet. "Troll feet can walk on anythin'," he said proudly. "We're made fer harsh weather."

Suddenly, from the side of the pond, something burst out of the snow. It flew through the air, disappeared back into the snow, then shot out again, hitting Merly in the stomach and knocking him down. This time they both recognized Senry's laugh.

"Look!" shouted Merly, still lying on his back. He had caught hold of the wriggling dea and now held it out to Ryah. It was made of something softer than clay. Softer and more durable, almost like real skin and fur. "Are they all like this?" he asked Senry.

"Probably," said Senry. "You'll have to wait till spring to find out fer sure."

"They are like plants," explained Eldamaea later. "Not sentient, but they will move and change. Those that keep my interest will stay and grow."

It was their last day together, for Ryah and her parents would be leaving in the morning, before the slopes became impassable. Their shoes were mended and provisions packed, and all the little details of leaving were wrapped up.

Senry was to accompany them. "I'll take the powder with me, but I won't be doin' any tradin' for a while. First, I'll meet with the council," he said, "and they with the citizens they represent. The townspeople will be given a choice to keep their deas free or not."

"I have been thinking," said Arn to Eldamaea that evening at a farewell dinner in the great room. "If you are willing, we might visit in the summer. Ryah could add to the courtyard and I could bring some deas from the town, the best I can find. I will bring my own deas, if my talents fully return, and I will bring the deas of others as well."

Ryah clasped her hands together and then covered her mouth, looking from the witch to her father and back again.

"You are welcome here," Eldamaea said, "and your deas are welcome here."

When morning and the time of departure came, Ryah clung to Merly like a vine to a tree.

"I have Trey," he reminded her, "and Senry. He'll be back in a few days. And summer will be here soon."

"I know," said Ryah. "But I will miss you. You are my best and only friend."

"'Best' I like, but not 'only.' You need to find a friend in your town. A friend among your own people."

Ryah scowled. "They are not my people. You are."

"Search, really search," Merly urged. "Hunt carefully and patiently. You might be surprised. Fer me, it was all or nothin'. But it doesn't have to be that way fer you."

Ryah didn't answer. The stubborn part of her didn't want any other friend. But a quieter, deeper part knew he was right.

When Ryah left with her family, Merly stood in the snow at the courtyard gate, twisting his sleeve around his finger till Ryah could no longer see him.

In the town, it was as Ryah's parents had described. Some delighted in the rediscovered complexities of living deas. Others longed for the order (and the profits) of the old days. Senry insisted that the council not vote alone, but that meetings be called so that all of the people would have a chance to voice their preference. In the end, the law was changed. There would be no more powder or pods or dead deas. But people were free to buy and sell their deas if they wished, though eventually the bliss of creating deas was known again by all.

Gradually, word spread among those who delighted most in the creative process that the witch on the mountain welcomed their talents and gifts. When Ryah and her parents set off for the fortress the following summer, they carried with them deas that were offered freely by others in their community, offered in the hope that they might take a place among the cherished deas of their fathers and their fathers' fathers high in the mountain shrine.

Today, the entire castle is a celebration of the magic of humans, the inspiration of trolls, the evolution of life unfettered. And the red bird sings.

About the Author

Valerie Tarico, Ph.D., is a practicing psychologist, journalist, and award-winning author and blogger. She graduated from Wheaton College, a Christian liberal arts college, and then she earned a doctorate in Counseling Psychology from the University of Iowa and completed postdoctoral studies at the University of Washington. She currently lives in Seattle, Washington with her husband and two daughters.

Dr. Tarico's first book, *Trusting Doubt: A Former Evangelical Looks at Old Beliefs in a New Light*, examines her early evangelical beliefs through the lens of her psychological training and life experience. *Trusting Doubt* was awarded a Silver medal in the Religion category at the Independent Publishers Book Awards.

Currently, Dr. Tarico writes for *The Huffington Post* and ExChristian.net, with an emphasis on helping others through the very personal and difficult process of expanding their spirituality beyond fundamentalist Christian doctrine. More broadly, Dr. Tarico is committed to promoting interfaith dialogue and the shared values which link all humanity. She speaks to churches and secular groups on topics such as moral development, the psychology of belief, and wisdom convergence. She also manages WisdomCommons.org, an interactive library of stories, poems, quotations, and essays about character virtues that are universally shared among secular, religious, and wisdom traditions.

About the Artist

Tony Troy was born in Liverpool, England, went to boarding school in Devon, then attended London University, where he obtained a bachelor's degree in Physics. With little ambition for the world of science, Mr. Troy bounced from one job to the next, until one day when he came across a group of street artist drawing portraits of tourists. Captivated, Mr. Troy paused to exchange words with one of the artists and share his dream of becoming an artist himself. Suddenly, the portraitist looked at his watch then hurried away, expressing the need to catch an evening flight to South Africa. "What about your gear?" Mr. Troy called out. The gear in question included two stools, a fine trestled easel, and numerous pencils and paper. "Too heavy to take on the plane, Mate," the street artist yelled back. "Tell you what … since you dream of being an artist, it's all yours!" So began a long and successful career in the arts.

To date, Mr. Troy has been featured at art shows in London, Paris, Rome, Copenhagen, and the United States. His portraits have been hung at The Royal Society of Portrait Painters and The Pastel Society in London. Currently, he accepts commissioned work and may be contacted for more information at his website: TonyTroyIllustrations.com.

In addition, Mr. Troy is an accomplished musician and playwright. His first musical, *The Flute Player's Song*, was successfully produced. The show was recorded and CDs are available at his website. Presently, Mr. Troy is seeking to take his musical to Broadway, and he continues to write music that inspires the body, mind, and spirit.

About the Publisher

The Truth:

The founders of The Oracle Institute are gravely concerned that the greatest crisis facing humanity is the resurgence of religious intolerance perpetrated in the name of God. We chose the Pentacle as our icon because, to us, this symbol represents the emerging spiritual unification of the five primary religions: Hinduism, Judaism, Buddhism, Christianity, and Islam. We believe the time has come for humanity to shed archaic belief systems about the Supreme Being, actively engage in interfaith dialogue, and prepare for the next phase of our collective spiritual evolution.

The Love:

The Oracle Institute promotes a process of soul growth which includes study, worship, meditation, and good works through application of the Golden Rule – what we refer to as the "Eleventh Commandment" brought by Jesus. When we earnestly strive to perfect ourselves, practice compassion toward our brothers and sisters, and assume responsibility for the health of our planet, we help birth a new spiritual paradigm.

The Light:

Many people are now ready to manifest "heaven on earth" – the prophesied era of abundance, peace, and harmony foretold by the prophets of every religion and the elders of every indigenous wisdom culture. To that end, The Oracle Institute offers interfaith books, spirituality classes, civics seminars, health and mindfulness programs, and holistic products designed to foster the quest for spiritual enlightenment.

We invite you to join us on our journey of Truth, Love, and Light

Donations may be made to:

The Oracle Institute
501(c)(3) educational charity
An Advocate for Enlightenment and a Vanguard for Spiritual Evolution

1990 Battlefield Drive
Independence, VA 24348
www.TheOracleInstitute.org

All donations and proceeds from our books and classes are used to further
Our educational mission and to build the Peace Pentagon:
An Interfaith and Social Justice Center in Independence, Virginia